For all readers,
young and old(er)

Matt Oldfield is a children's author focusing on the wonderful world of football. His other books include *Unbelievable Football* (winner of the 2020 Children's Sports Book of the Year) and the *Johnny Ball: Football Genius* series. In association with his writing, Matt also delivers writing workshops in schools.

Cover illustration by Dan Leydon.
To learn more about Dan visit danleydon.com
To purchase his artwork visit etsy.com/shop/footynews
Or just follow him on Twitter @danleydon

TABLE OF CONTENTS

ACKNOWLEDGEMENTS

First of all I'd like to thank everyone at Bonnier Books, especially Saaleh Patel, for supporting me and for running the ever-expanding UFH ship so smoothly. Writing stories for the next generation of football fans is both an honour and a pleasure. Thanks also to my agent, Nick Walters, for helping to keep my dream job going, year after year.

Next up, an extra big cheer for all the teachers, booksellers and librarians who have championed these books, and, of course, for the readers. The success of this series is truly down to you.

Okay, onto friends and family. I wouldn't be writing this series if it wasn't for my brother Tom. I owe him so much and I'm very grateful for his belief in me as an author. I'm also very grateful to the rest of my family, especially Mel, Noah, Nico, and of course Mum and Dad. To my parents, I owe my biggest passions: football and books. They're a real inspiration for everything I do.

Pang, Will, Mills, Doug, Naomi, John, Charlie, Sam, Katy, Ben, Karen, Ana (and anyone else I forgot) – thanks for all the love and laughs, but sorry, no I won't be getting 'a real job' anytime soon!

And finally, I couldn't have done any of this without Iona's encouragement and understanding. Much love to you, and of course to Arlo, the ultimate hero of all. I hope we get to enjoy these books together one day.

CHAPTER 1

SO CLOSE TO EURO GLORY

11 July 2021, Wembley Stadium

It's coming home, it's coming home, it's coming,
FOOTBALL'S COMING HOME!'

The Euro 2020 final was finally here, and the England fans were cranking up the noise around Wembley. In the tunnel, Declan Rice joined his teammates, all of them looking restless with a mix of nerves and fired-up energy. Already he could hear the famous 'Three Lions' song belting around the stadium. Despite the focus and intensity that he was feeling, the song always made him smile.

'We're one big performance away from doing it and lifting the trophy,' he reminded himself quietly. It was fifty-five years since England had won a major international tournament, but here they were ahead of their final test against a strong Italy team.

At last, there was the clatter of studs ahead of him and the line was moving. He heard the booming stadium speakers announce that the teams were on their way and, seconds later, he emerged onto the Wembley pitch with roars coming from all corners of the stadium.

After all the preparation, with the goosebumps from the national anthem and the energy surging through his body, Declan tried to stay composed. England boss Gareth Southgate and the coaching staff had made that point again and again: don't let the big occasion take you out of your usual rhythm.

Declan squeezed in a couple more stretches and jumped in the air to win an imaginary header. This was the biggest game of his life – and he couldn't wait to get stuck in.

He saw Harry Kane walking towards the centre

circle for the coin toss, and gave him a fist bump on the way. 'Do what you do best today, Dec,' Harry said. 'Win tackles, shut down the space and get us moving forward.'

This moment, and everything from the team's Euro 2020 run, was even more special for Declan with Mason Mount playing just in front of him in the England midfield. The two inseparable childhood friends had shared in so much of each other's journeys – and, together, they now had a chance to fire England to Euro 2020 glory.

'It doesn't get any better than this!' Declan shouted, making himself heard over all the noise.

'Let's do this!' Mason yelled back, with a big grin on his face. They were both determined to enjoy today, despite the high stakes. Declan gave him a high-five and jogged back into position.

Just as Gareth had wanted, England came flying out of the traps. Declan shadowed the Italy midfielders and gave them no space to take a touch. In no time, Kieran Trippier was surging down the right wing. Declan watched as Kieran's cross floated into the box, almost in slow motion, and landed at the back post.

Declan felt his heart skip a beat as Luke Shaw appeared. He was unmarked! Luke took the shot first time, and Declan leapt in the air as the ball clipped the post and flew into the net. 1–0!

Wembley was rocking. Even with all Italy's experience, Declan could see England's start had rattled them. 'Don't ease up now!' he called to his teammates after racing back and winning a header.

But Italy fought back in the second half. Suddenly, England were camped in their own half, and Declan was finding it tougher to relieve the pressure on the defence.

'If we can just get through this tricky patch, we'll be fine,' he called to Mason as they waited for a goal kick.

Moments later, though, Wembley fell silent – with the exception of the Italy fans. England failed to deal with a corner and the ball was in the net before any of the white shirts could recover. 1–1.

Declan pulled up his socks and shook off the disappointment. There were still more than twenty minutes to regain control. He set the tone with one thundering tackle, winning the ball fairly and getting the England fans on their feet again.

But with just over fifteen minutes left, Gareth decided to freshen up the midfield, bringing on Jordan Henderson. There was nothing Declan wanted more than to keep battling alongside his teammates, but he was the man being subbed off. He jogged off, trying his best to hide the disappointment. 'Good luck, Hendo,' he said, high-fiving him on the touchline.

If going toe-to-toe against the Italy midfield seemed like a draining task, watching the rest of the final from the bench was even harder. As the game went into extra-time, Mason was soon next to Declan as Gareth made more changes. Together, they bit their fingernails, willing every England attack to strike a knockout blow.

When the final whistle blew, the tension tripled around Wembley. Declan and Mason looked at each other. 'Penalties,' they both said at the same moment, puffing out their cheeks and taking a deep breath.

Gareth confirmed the order of the penalty

takers, and Declan joined in with the cheers of encouragement. Now all he could do was watch. It started so well, with Jordan Pickford saving Italy's second penalty. Declan allowed himself a quick fist pump. Advantage, England!

But the mood quickly turned. Declan felt his stomach churn and then sink as England missed their last three penalties. The Italian celebrations began just yards away, leaving Declan and his teammates to process the shock. England had been so close to finally ending the long trophy drought, but it had slipped through their fingers.

There would be time to dwell on all the 'what ifs' later, but now Declan's main concern was putting an arm round the players dealing with the pain of missing their penalties. 'We win together and we lose together,' he told them. 'You were brave enough to take one. Keep your head up.'

Back in the dressing room, Declan felt the heartbreak hit him even harder. The tears flowed and he stayed in his kit for what felt like hours. But the more he reflected on the past month and on the words of encouragement that Gareth shared with the team, the more another emotion burst through alongside the sadness: pride.

Declan was so proud of what England had achieved over the past few weeks – and the central role that he had played in the team as a twenty-two-year-old. After finally getting changed, he stood in front of one of the dressing room mirrors to adjust his collar. 'We'll be back... and better than ever,' he said to himself.

As Declan had proved many times already in his short career, he was an unstoppable force when he set his mind on something.

CHAPTER 2

KING OF THE KINGSTON STREETS

'Dec, you're on my team,' called Connor.

Little Declan's eyes lit up. He grinned at his brother, then scurried over to drop off his school bag next to all the others.

Deep down, Declan knew that he was mainly being picked because there weren't as many players today for the daily street football game just round the corner from the Rice family's home in Kingston upon Thames in south-west London. But he didn't care. Declan just wanted to show that, even though he was still only seven years old, he could battle the older boys.

Connor and Jordan, Declan's other brother, were

regulars in these games. 'If you can survive out here, eleven-a-side football will be a breeze,' they liked to say,

'Watch out for the little guy!' shouted Danny, one of the older boys in the same class as Connor. He laughed, clearly thinking Declan would be no threat at all. A few of the others joined in, giggling loudly.

'Ignore him,' Connor said quietly, putting an arm round his little brother. 'Just get stuck in.'

Declan started off playing in defence. He listened to the calls from his teammates – when to push up, who to mark, where to stand. So far, he seemed to be doing fine.

Then a long pass bounced past two of his teammates and Liam, another of the older boys, was through on goal. Declan spotted the danger and sprinted as fast as he could. Liam thought he had all the time in the world to line up his shot, but Declan appeared out of nowhere to get his foot in front of the ball and deflect it wide of the 'post' (one pile of bags).

'Nice one, Dec!' yelled Jordan, rushing over to give his brother a quick hug. 'That's how it's done, boys.'

Declan felt like he was flying now. He buzzed around, feeling more confident and calling for passes. He smiled as his teammates began to trust him with the ball. One pass took an awkward bounce off his shin, but he was fast enough to recover and skip past one tackle. Danny lunged in but Declan was expecting it. He just prodded the ball through Danny's legs and kept running. 'Megs!' he shouted, before setting up Connor for a tap-in.

'Lucky!' he heard Danny muttering.

The ball was like a magnet, and some of the other boys were backing off warily. None of them wanted to be embarrassed by 'the little kid'.

'Is he really only seven?' Danny asked Connor when they all finally stopped for a water break.

Declan saw Connor nod. 'And he's fearless!' Connor added.

As Declan walked over, Danny looked up and gave him a high-five. 'Fair play,' Danny said. 'That was an impressive run!'

Declan did his best to play it cool, but a smile quickly spread across his face. 'Thanks,' he replied.

'These games are even more fun than I was expecting.'

That evening, Declan replayed his highlights for anyone who would listen. His mum, Teresa, smiled patiently every time he hopped up from the table to repeatedly show exactly how he had made the big tackle and played the perfect pass.

'I'm proud of you, darling,' she said. 'Good for you for taking on the bigger boys. As long as you're being really careful and looking out for cars and bikes, maybe you can join your brothers again tomorrow.'

In the past, that kind of suggestion might have been met with eye-rolling and sarcastic comments from his brothers about how embarrassing it would be to have Declan there. But, to his surprise, Jordan and Connor both nodded. He had passed the test!

The next day, he was back there with his brothers and, even though there were more players, no-one sent him away. Week after week, he was in the thick of the action, not willing to give an inch, even when the older boys towered over him.

Even though he still preferred to stay in defence, his passing and shooting quickly improved – and

soon no-one needed to tell Declan who to mark or
where to be.

CHAPTER 3

A HELPING HAND FROM FAMILY

'I can't wait to see Taylor again!' Declan said, sitting down for a quick breakfast before catching up with his cousin. Teresa put a plate of toast on the table and smiled.

'Just remember that Taylor is the one playing in the tournament and you're there to watch,' she reminded him. 'Stay with Uncle Nick on the touchline.'

Declan laughed but promised to behave. He would have loved to get on the pitch, even for just a few minutes. Taylor was currently playing for the Chelsea Under 14s and today he would be taking on academy teams from across the country.

When Uncle Nick honked the horn, Declan

bounded down to the car with his ball under his arm. He tried not to ask too many questions on the drive, but still got a few funny stories out of Taylor about life at the academy.

Seeing Taylor and the other Chelsea players warming up and wearing the famous blue shirt, Declan stood silently and soaked up every minute. He wanted to get all the little details right when he told his school friends about this experience.

He and Taylor had played in a few games together with friends and family in the summer. His cousin was a really good player, but Declan had earned Taylor's respect with some nice touches.

'Good win, buddy!' he called out as Taylor jogged over after one of the tournament games – an easy 4–0 win for Chelsea. 'You smashed 'em.'

Taylor guzzled some water and tucked into an orange slice. Clearly, this was all normal for him. But Declan was buzzing. He dribbled a ball around, trying out some of the tricks he had seen at the tournament so far.

'That move you did on the wing was amazing!' he

told Taylor. 'The defender tripped over his own feet when you changed direction. Your Number 8 did a crazy stepover in that last game too. I'm loving this!'

'You can do all those things too,' Taylor said, looking over at his cousin.

Declan shrugged. 'Maybe on my best days. But you all make it look so easy.'

'Well, we've had a few more years of practice. Trust me, you're ahead of where I was at your age.'

This was probably the highlight of the day so far for Declan. He really looked up to Taylor and knew his cousin wouldn't say something like that unless he meant it.

'You would be great in these types of games,' Taylor continued. 'I was thinking in the car... do you want me to see if I can get you a trial at Chelsea with the Under-8s?'

'Are you serious?' Declan asked, feeling his legs go all shaky.

'Sure. I can talk to one of my coaches and find out who to ask. No guarantees, but I'll do my best.'

Declan grinned and nodded. Then he went silent for

a few minutes. Taylor got up to rejoin his teammates and prepare for the next knockout game. As much as Declan tried to remind himself that there was only a slim chance that Taylor would be able to set something up, his mind wandered. What would it be like to wear the Chelsea shirt in a youth tournament? What would it be like for his family of Chelsea fans? He was still closely watching Taylor's knockout round games, but he had an extra burst of energy as he worked on his keepy-ups on the touchline.

A week later, Teresa appeared in the living room doorway, signalling for Declan to come to the phone. 'It's Taylor,' she whispered, handing the phone carefully to her son.

'Hey, Dec, it's your agent,' Taylor said, laughing and then sensing Declan's confusion. 'The trial – remember? I asked one of the coaches this week and he wants to see you play. He was thinking of coming to see one of your club games, but you're not playing for anyone, are you?'

Declan's heart sank. He understood his parents' decision not to join a local club team, given some of their experiences with Jordan and Connor in the local leagues, but now he feared it might cost him an amazing chance at Chelsea. 'Ah, no I'm not.'

'But don't panic yet,' Taylor continued. 'My dad is going to speak with them as well to see what they can arrange.'

That made Declan feel a bit better. If he could just get the chance to show what he could do, he was sure that he could impress the Chelsea coaches.

The next surprise phone call wasn't from Taylor. This time, it was from the Chelsea academy. Declan had explained the whole story to his parents after Taylor's last update, but his dad still sounded surprised. 'Chelsea academy,' he mouthed silently to Teresa and Declan, who were sitting at the kitchen table working on his homework. They sat up in shock.

Declan could only hear one side of the conversation, so he tried to watch his dad's facial expressions for clues instead. At one point, his dad seemed to be scribbling something on a piece of paper, but he was too far away to see what it was.

Sean ended the call and slowly put the phone back

in its usual place. He turned to face Declan, who was wriggling impatiently in his chair.

'Well, Taylor was right,' Sean explained. 'They're keen to see you in action but…'

Declan looked at the ground. 'I know, I know,' he mumbled. 'They can't move forward with a trial because I don't play for a team.'

'Hang on, let me finish,' Sean said, a serious look now giving way to a smile. 'They've got some trials coming up but they're also running a mini training session with a few of boys in the Under-8 and Under-9 age groups. They suggested that we bring you to that as a kind of pre-trial.'

Declan's eyes filled with hope again. 'What?! When?'

'Next Thursday at seven. I've got all the details right here.'

Declan bounced up the stairs two at a time. Maybe there was still a chance for this Chelsea dream.

The pre-trial went as well as he could have hoped. There were a few passing drills at the start, and then a series of 3-on-3 games, with boys swapping in and out constantly. By the end, he was sweating heavily in the summer heat but felt proud of his performance.

The Chelsea coaches split up and began making their way around the group of parents on the touchline. Declan waited patiently next to his dad, too tired to do much more than drink his water.

Soon, it was Declan's turn. One of the coaches wandered over, shook hands and got straight to the point. 'Declan did really well today – good technique, good movement, incredible energy. We'd like to see him at the trial later this month.'

It was a short conversation, but that was all Declan needed to hear. While his dad got the information about the trial and confirmed all the right contact details, Declan treated himself to a few minutes of rest on the grass. 'I've earned that at least,' he thought, grinning and wiping the sweat from his eyes.

CHAPTER 4

CHAPTER 4

TRIAL TIME!

Declan hardly slept the night before his Chelsea trial. He woke at 10pm, then fell back asleep. He stirred again at 2am, feeling suddenly wide awake, but it was way too early to think about breakfast. The pattern continued at 4am and 5am.

Finally, his alarm clock showed 6:30am and Declan decided there was little chance of getting any more sleep. He tiptoed out of his room and down the stairs. His stomach was doing cartwheels. He turned on the TV and lay down on the sofa.

Even though no-one was pushing Declan to get into the Chelsea academy, he still felt some pressure. He didn't want to let Taylor down after his cousin had persuaded the coaches to give Declan this chance, and he knew how cool it would be for his parents and brothers to have this special connection to their favourite team. Most of all, he really wanted to test himself against other good players.

But he brushed those thoughts aside. His dad's number one message for Declan, Connor and Jordan had always been centred around enjoying their football. It was a game – and they should have fun playing it. 'I just need to think of it like that,' Declan said quietly to himself.

Declan had only told a couple of his friends about the trial – just in case it turned out to be a disaster. The Chelsea coaches had confirmed that he could turn up in whatever kit he wanted, so Declan chose one of his old (but lucky!) Chelsea home shirts. That blue matched some of the designs on his new boots, which he had been busy getting used to over the last few days to avoid any unwanted blisters.

The drive to the training ground was a fairly short one, but it still felt like an eternity to Declan. He peered out of the window as his dad finally parked the car right next to one of the pitches. A few forms and a few handshakes later, Declan was in a crowded changing room being introduced to some of the other Under-8s.

His nerves quickly wore off once he was standing in a small group passing a ball back and forth. He watched in awe at some of the other boys' skills and footwork, and tried to remember that his game was about more than fancy flicks. He could win headers, crunch into tackles and run tirelessly.

'Sorry, these are the rules,' one of the Chelsea academy boys said, grinning and holding out a stack of cones. 'We all had to do it at our first trial session. Just use the cones to split the penalty area into three separate zones.'

Declan laughed. 'Fair enough,' he said, taking the cones and accepting a fist bump. Then, with a wink, he added: 'Is there a record time for setting them up?'

This was all new territory for Declan. He was sure that most of the other boys had played for local teams before being scouted for the academy – and that meant they had been through all kinds of training drills, stretches and mini-games.

But nevertheless, Declan managed to figure it out. His first touch was sharp, and he listened carefully to the coaches to make sure he understood the different drills. That was no easy task, as some of the drills involved multiple layers of instructions – dribble around the first cone, then up to the second cone, lay it off to the left and join the back of the line to the right. Declan soaked it all in and tried to visualize each step.

For the mini-games, he was handed a green bib along with four of the other boys. 'We're going to dominate!' one of the boys said. 'Declan, right? I'm Mason Mount.'

Declan smiled a little shyly and shook his hand. One of the coaches wheeled over medium-sized goals and placed them at either end of a shortened pitch. Another coach grabbed the nearest ball, punted it high into the air and shouted 'Play!'

Even with a goalkeeper on each team, there was limited space for a five-a-side game. But it encouraged two-touch passing and good movement. That suited

Declan just fine. He dropped deeper, called for the ball, then swept a pass over to Mason. He darted forward, this time into a small pocket of space, and got the ball again. Just like his brothers had always taught him, Declan already had his next pass planned before the ball arrived at his feet. With a quick drop of the shoulder, he created room for a lay-off to Steve, a tall, skinny defender.

The give-and-go style was fun, but eventually Declan decided to be more adventurous. With the other team starting to get comfortable closing down the space for short passes, he jogged towards Mason. 'Cut it back!' he shouted.

Mason pinged a quick pass to Declan, who controlled it instantly. But instead of another little flick to Steve, who was within five yards of him, he did what the defenders were least expecting. He took one positive touch forward with his right foot and, sensing the space opening up, unleashed a swerving shot. It felt good as soon as it left his boot – and the 'thump' sounded good too. He looked up to see the ball soaring towards the net, then dipping into the top corner.

Goooooooooooooooooooooaaaaaaaaaaaaaaaallllllllllllll llllllllllll!!!!!!!!!!!!!!!!!!!!

Declan instinctively put his arm in the air to celebrate, before hurriedly pulling it down by his side. It was probably better to make it look like he was used to scoring these types of goal, he thought.

'Woah!!!' Mason screamed. 'That's a worldie!'

There were oohs and aahs from the coaches too – all of whom seemed to be glued to watching Declan's game now. His confidence was sky high, but he kept reminding himself what he did best. Sure, it was special to smash in a screamer like that. But he spent the next twenty minutes showing off all his other skills. He cleared one attack with a diving header, slid in to win the ball back near the touchline, and somehow still had enough energy to race into the box to get on the end of a cross.

There was a lot of excitement among the Chelsea coaches. 'That's a good sign,' Mason told Declan quietly as they both watched the far touchline. 'You're doing something right if they're all comparing notes and passing papers around.'

Michael Beale, one of the academy coaches, had seen enough to know he had a gem here. When Sean brought over Declan's water bottle and put his arm round his son, Michael was quickly on the scene to start up a conversation.

'Declan really looked at home with the other lads,' he began, fidgeting a little with excitement. 'He's the full package and we'd love to have him at Chelsea. Do you have fifteen minutes to go over the forms and get everything signed?'

Just like that? Declan thought to himself, with his mouth wide open. He had assumed the trial period would last multiple weeks.

Sean paused. 'Let me just talk to Declan first. Can we meet you over at the reception area?'

'Sure, no problem. Take your time.'

Once the coaches were out of earshot, Sean turned to Declan. 'So, what do you reckon? I think I already know the answer, but did you have a good time out there?'

'No, Dad, I had a great time!' Declan replied, laughing. 'But thanks for letting this be my decision.

If you and Mum are okay with it, I'd love to join the Chelsea academy.'

'Alright, let's do this!' Sean said, putting his arm round Declan and pretending to flex his writing hand ready to sign the forms.

While he would never admit that he was tired, Declan really had to drag himself over to the car when it was time to leave. But, with a brown envelope next to him on the back seat with their copies of the signed academy forms, he rested his head happily against the window for most of the drive home.

CHAPTER 5

BEST BUDS

'Does Mason know that we're taking the family Christmas photo at the weekend?' Jordan joked as Declan and Mason wheeled their bikes round to the side of the house and leaned them against the wall before dinner.

'We should probably put out an extra plate for Christmas lunch too!' Sean joined in.

Declan laughed, elbowing Mason playfully in the ribs. 'See, just like I told you. You're basically my third brother!'

Ever since Declan's first few weeks of training with the Chelsea academy, Mason – or 'Mase' – had become an honorary member of the Rice family. The two boys were inseparable – and, if they weren't out on their bikes or playing video games at Declan's house, they were doing the same thing at Mason's house.

Once Declan had officially joined the academy, he and Mason saw each other four days a week for training, and they were often the first two boys to arrive. Kicking the ball back and forth on the AstroTurf while they waited, they struck up a fast friendship.

As Teresa and Sean brought in the plates of piping hot food, Mason tapped Declan on the shoulder. 'Have you shown them your Beckham impression?' he asked.

This was Declan's latest party trick. He loved doing impressions of famous people – and he was actually pretty good at them. Launching into a Beckham speech about winning the Treble, Mason giggled and almost fell off his chair. 'That's so good!'

Declan's family knew from experience that it was never just one impression. Sure enough, it shifted from Beckham to Rio Ferdinand to Wayne Rooney and so on. Teresa watched her son milking the attention and joining in the laughter, and she was pleased to see a smile on Declan's face, easing her own worries about the toll it was taking on him to train so many evenings a week on top of full days at school. She had become friends with Mason's mum over the past few months – and she knew that their drive up from Portsmouth four days a week couldn't be easy either.

Even though he had settled in well at the academy, Declan's head was still spinning. There had been so many jaw-dropping moments already at Chelsea but, as one of the newer players in his age group, he felt some added pressure to prove himself to the coaches.

It helped to have Mason there, living the same experiences and riding the same rollercoaster of emotions. Declan was on top of the world after a good training session, then back to questioning whether he belonged when he was below his usual standards.

'I love being part of the academy, but sometimes it's so strange to think about how different our life is compared to other boys our age,' Declan told Mason breathlessly as he tried to get maximum airtime on Mason's trampoline the following week.

'Yeah, it definitely makes us grow up faster,' Mason

replied, doing some keepy-ups while waiting for his turn.

'So many of the boys and girls at school ask what it's like, but it's so hard to understand the whole experience unless you're living it,' Declan added. 'I've had people asking if we train with Drogba and Lampard, or whether we play our games at Stamford Bridge!'

Mason laughed. 'I get some interesting questions too! Last week, a boy asked me if I'd be inviting any of the Chelsea players to my birthday party. I didn't want to make him feel bad, so I just said "maybe".'

Declan was giggling so much that he almost mistimed his landing and fell off the trampoline. 'Your party is going to be the hottest ticket in town!'

'Whatever happens with our careers, let's promise to always have each other's back,' Declan added. 'I'm sure there are going to be lots more twists and turns for both of us.'

'Deal, mate,' Mason replied. 'Then, one day, we'll be on the pitch together in the Premier League. I really believe that.'

Declan leapt into the air again. He was just glad to have a friend who did understand.

CHAPTER 6

SQUEEZING IN SCHOOL GAMES

On Declan's first day at Grey Court School, football was unsurprisingly the main topic of conversation. The school had a proud reputation on the pitch and there was already lots of chatter about who would make the football team.

'I can't wait for the trials!' a boy named Sam said excitedly. 'I've been playing for my local team for the last four years, usually in defence.'

'I'm a winger,' added another voice – a small, skinny boy called Wayne. 'I'm not the strongest but I'm really fast.'

Declan stayed silent. He didn't want to sound like a show-off in his first week at a new school by talking about life at the Chelsea academy. Still, he wasn't going to lie about it either.

Sam turned to him suddenly. 'What about you, Declan?' he asked. 'Do you play for a team?'

Declan could feel his cheeks going red. He smiled a little nervously. 'Yeah, I do. Usually in midfield, but sometimes at centre back.'

'It's good to be able to play a few positions,' Wayne joined in. 'I'm sure the school coaches will like that.'

'Who do you play for?' Sam said while reaching into his locker to grab a textbook.

'Erm... Chelsea,' Declan answered.

Sam dropped the textbook and almost hit his head on the door of his locker. 'What?!'

Declan wasn't sure what to say next – and he was still laughing about Sam's dramatic reaction. Wayne and Sam started laughing too. 'Good one!' Wayne called, as they walked off to their first class of the day.

'I wasn't joking!' Declan mumbled to himself, shaking his head.

He was shaking his head again later that week when the details for the football team trials were posted on the main sports noticeboard. The trials would be happening at the same time as his Chelsea training session.

That evening, Declan gobbled down his supper but hardly said a word. 'What's wrong, son?' his dad asked, reaching over and putting a hand on his head. 'Not feeling well?'

'No, I'm fine,' Declan said. 'But I'm going to miss the school football trials next week. We'll be in the car on the way to Chelsea training.'

His parents both gave him a sympathetic look. 'I know that must sting,' his dad replied. 'But maybe it's a good thing. There's only so much football you can squeeze into each week, and we've talked about how you may have to sacrifice certain things because of your commitment to Chelsea.'

That didn't help Declan's mood. 'Yeah, but the other kids don't even believe that I play for Chelsea,' he snapped. 'I bet they'll think I'm skipping the trials because I don't think I can get into the team. They've only ever seen me kick the ball around in the playground.'

Sure enough, the day after the trial, Sam jogged over to Declan's locker at the morning break. 'Hi, mate,' he said, patting his new friend on the back. 'Where were you yesterday? We thought you'd be at the trials.'

Declan paused. 'I had training at the Chelsea academy at the exact same time and I couldn't skip that,' he eventually replied.

Sam looked at him for a few seconds without saying a word. 'You're serious about being at Chelsea?' he said, with a frown. 'We thought it was just a wind-up.'

Declan laughed. 'So do you believe me now? Or do I have to run rings round you on the pitch first?'

While his friends started to see more and more of his skills in the playground games at lunchtimes, Declan's next task was convincing the coaches to change the usual kick-off times. By now, the Grey Court coaches had seen Declan play in enough school practices to know that he was the type of rare talent that could carry the school to local and regional trophies.

'Mr Willmore, my mum picks me up for training straight after school,' he pleaded. 'I'll never be able to play in a game at 4:30. What would it take to move kick-offs to 3:30?'

Mr Willmore knew it would be an unusual step – and an unpopular one for some at the school – but perhaps not impossible. He promised to look into it. To Declan's surprise, the coaches found a way to change the kick-off time.

To make this work, Declan knew every minute would count. 'Mum, can I have pasta in the car on the way to training?' he asked, standing in the kitchen doorway. 'Then we can leave straight from school and save some time.'

Jordan and Connor laughed loudly in the living room. 'He's got a more packed schedule than the Prime Minister!' Jordan shouted.

'I'll do whatever it takes to play!' Declan called, sprinting up the stairs to get his shin pads.

The next morning, he hopped out of bed, instantly feeling wide awake. Today was the day – his first game for Grey Court, back to back with another training session at Chelsea. As planned, he guzzled down a tall glass of water in the kitchen, then prepared a big bowl of cereal. He was going to need every ounce of energy.

Declan gave his teachers his full attention all morning but, by early afternoon, his mind had drifted to the upcoming game. As he joined his teammates in the school changing room, Mr Willmore dropped off the kits. Declan scooped up a shirt, shorts and socks, putting them on one of the benches and sitting down to admire the blue-and-yellow shirt.

This first game proved to be one-sided from the very start. Within the first two minutes, Declan won a tackle in midfield and played a through ball for Wayne to chase. Racing up in support, Declan called for the cutback and then swept a left-footed shot into the bottom corner.

Goooooooooooooooooooooaaaaaaaaaaaaaaaaalllllllllllllll lllllllllllll!!!!!!!!!!!!!!!!!!!!!!

Two minutes later, Declan went on a mazy dribble before teeing up Freddie, one of the Grey Court strikers, for a simple tap-in. On the touchline, Mr Willmore had to look away to hide his grin as the opposition coach slapped his thighs in frustration.

Declan was soon on the move again. He pressured one of the defenders into a bad touch, took the ball, then danced past two tackles and curled a shot from outside the box beyond the goalkeeper's dive.

Goooooooooooooooooooaaaaaaaaaaaaaaaaalllllllllllllll llllllllllll!!!!!!!!!!!!!!!!!!!!!

'There's the Chelsea magic!' Sam called, running over and jumping on Declan's back. 'You're making this look way too easy!'

At the start of the second half, Declan set up two more goals, then went searching for his hat-trick. Sam's long clearance bounced nicely for Freddie, who held off one defender and poked a hopeful cross into the box. Declan timed his run perfectly and got in front of his marker to calmly stroke the ball into the net.

Goooooooooooooooooooaaaaaaaaaaaaaaaaalllllllllllllll llllllllllll!!!!!!!!!!!!!!!!!!!!!

A hat-trick in his first game for Grey Court!

Mr Willmore decided that his team had heaped enough misery on the opposition now. The next time the ball went out for a throw-in, he signalled to the referee and brought Declan off.

'I thought I should probably keep you fresh for
Chelsea,' Mr Willmore said quietly, when Declan
looked a bit disappointed to come off.

Declan nodded. He understood – and this would
help him get ready faster at the end of the game. Until
then, he could sit back and watch his teammates.

After a two-minute shower, Declan put his uniform
back on and waved a quick goodbye to his friends.
With his dad sailing through friendly traffic, he
changed into his Chelsea training kit on the way and
still arrived at the academy five minutes early.

He was full of confidence after the school game
and drilled his first two shots into the top corner
while he waited on the pitch with the other boys.
'You're looking sharp tonight, Declan!' called one of
the coaches. 'Whatever pre-training warm-up you're
doing, it's working!'

As Declan dribbled the ball back to the edge of box
for another shot, he covered his mouth to hide the
sneaky smile. So far, so good!

CHAPTER 7

TOURNAMENT TESTS

'I could get used to this!' Declan said happily as he reclined his seat and settled in for the flight to the Netherlands.

Next to him, as always, was Mason. Both boys had been picked in the Chelsea squad to represent the club at the Venlo Under-13s tournament, and they couldn't wait to test themselves against other top young players from across Europe.

'I know!' Mason replied. 'Just for today, we get to see what it's like to be Lampard or Hazard. We're living the pro life!'

Declan settled into his hotel room and let his parents know that he had arrived safely. One glance at the Chelsea itinerary on the little desk in the far corner of the room confirmed that it would be a busy week. In fact, they had a training session starting in a couple of hours.

A team lunch was served up in the main hotel meeting room, giving Declan a chance to catch up with the other boys. Some of them had played in the tournament the year before and were swapping stories about how close they had come to lifting the trophy.

With the tournament looming, there was some uncertainty for Declan over what position he would be playing, but he just focused on doing his best in training as Michael oversaw the sessions.

The uncertainty was resolved the next day when the coaches revealed the team for the opening group game. Declan was starting in central midfield!

He rushed back to his room to call his family and share the good news.

'I had no idea if I'd be playing or carrying the water bottles,' he said. 'But I'll be in midfield with Mason for the first game.'

'Wow!' he heard his mum say. 'Congratulations,

Dec! That's amazing!'

All the years spent on the same pitch together gave Declan and Mason an extra edge. Declan still wasn't the tallest, but he was a fearless tackler and always seemed to be in the right place to intercept passes. Once he got the ball back, he and Mason were always on the same wavelength. Without even needing to look up, it was like Declan had a special tracking device for finding Mason. Time and again, they surprised opponents with lightning counter-attacks.

The tournament definitely wasn't a holiday. Declan, Mason and the other boys all trained harder than ever as they tried to make their case to the coaches. Ahead of the semi-final against Anderlecht, Declan had heard rumours about one of their midfielders, who many of the top clubs in Europe were linked with. He spotted him during the warm-up and signalled to Mason. 'That's him – Number 7,' he said quietly.

Declan knew that Chelsea had to win that battle to have any chance of reaching the final – and he was up for the challenge. As the ball went out of play for the first throw-in of the game, Declan jogged to his left.

'I've got Number 7,' he shouted, pointing for Mason to mark the other central midfielder.

For the next ninety minutes, Declan shadowed Number 7 everywhere, climbing highest to win headers and sneaking in front of him to intercept passes. He watched the opposition's body language with a big grin on his face. Without their star man running the show, they were struggling to come up with a back-up plan.

Chelsea managed to grind out a 2–0 win and the coaches were just as excited as the players. Declan saw one of his coaches jump and punch the air twice at the final whistle. 'You set the tone for us,' another coach told Declan. 'Is Number 7 still in your pocket?' he added, pretending to check Declan's non-existent pockets.

As Declan caught his breath and drank more water, Chelsea had the Venlo final to prepare for. 'Let's nail the basics that got us here,' Michael said, leading the pre-game team talk. 'Keep your heads and make them play at our pace.'

The final was a stalemate, with neither team giving

an inch, even as legs and minds got increasingly tired. A penalty shootout would decide it. As Declan and his teammates huddled together on the pitch, he visualised what he was going to do. Hard and low to the keeper's left, he thought to himself.

When it came to his turn, no-one had missed yet. Declan brushed off the pressure, placed the ball on the spot and took a long look at the goal. With no hesitation, he ran up and steered his penalty past the goalkeeper's dive. He didn't want to over-celebrate, but he allowed himself a quick fist pump.

He rolled down his socks and stood with his teammates to watch the rest of the shootout. But the penalties kept flying in and suddenly they were going through the team for a second time. Then finally a miss. As Declan picked up the ball and placed it carefully on the spot, he now had a chance to win it. But this time he didn't have a clear plan. He just went for power.

As Declan looked up, he saw the ball sailing over the bar. He put his hands over his face and walked slowly back to the centre circle to join his teammates.

'Unlucky, Dec,' Mason said quietly.

Declan just shook his head and looked at the ground. He didn't want to talk to anyone at the moment. But his mood soon improved. Jamie, the Chelsea goalkeeper, scored his penalty, then dived to his right to make a spectacular save.

When Chelsea's winning penalty rocketed into the net, Declan and Mason jumped in the air and sprinted over to Jamie. 'You little legend!' Declan yelled as they all piled on top of their keeper.

The trophy presentation was even better than Declan had imagined. He received his medal from one of the tournament organisers and then joined his teammates to celebrate with the trophy. A few of the coaches pulled out their phones and took photos to share with all the parents.

'Can you take one of Mase and I?' Declan called out, with the trophy proudly in his hands. He and Mason put an arm round each other, with one hand each on the trophy. Declan grinned. 'Football is the best!' he said, already excited to share the news with his family.

The Venlo experience was just one of several youth team trophies for Declan and Mason as the Chelsea academy made its mark in England and across Europe. 'Now that I've got a taste for winning tournaments, I don't ever want to stop!' he told his brothers that summer. 'Luckily, there's plenty more chances ahead.'

CHAPTER 8

COUNTY CUP MAGIC

'This is the big one!' Sam called out as the Grey Court boys filed onto the bus for their Surrey County Cup showdown against Whitgift School. 'Dec, we'll need a monster performance from you today.'

Declan had a focused look on his face. He smiled for an instant, but then went back to staring out of the window. 'I'm ready,' he said. He was often quiet in the build-up to a game. It helped him clear his mind and forget any worries that were burdening him.

Plus, there were major bragging rights on the line. He knew a couple of the Chelsea boys who went to Whitgift and a few others who were at the Crystal Palace academy. It was the sort of game that got the scouts excited.

He jogged from one side of the pitch to the other during the warm-up, and he waved to a few of the Whitgift boys that he knew. But he knew he had to put friendships aside for the next ninety minutes.

The momentum swung back and forth, with the two teams bringing out the best in each other. With the game hanging in the balance, Declan saw Sam bundled over in the box.

'Penalty!' Declan shouted, joining the chorus of other Grey Court voices.

The referee hesitated then blew his whistle, signalling for a penalty.

'You've got this, Dec!' yelled Mr Willmore, offering a thumbs-up as he paced along the touchline.

Declan nodded and walked forward to get the ball. He placed it carefully on the penalty spot and took five steps backwards for his run-up. The Whitgift goalkeeper was moving around on his goal line, trying all kinds of distracting movements to put him off. Declan took a deep breath, looked down at the ground and waited.

He heard the referee's whistle and ran forward confidently, trying not to give away his plan to shoot to the goalkeeper's right. Declan planted his left foot and swung through hard with his right. The connection felt good – but had he hit it too well?

Declan glanced up to see his penalty soaring higher than he intended – but not over the bar; just into the top corner. The goalkeeper had dived the wrong way.

Goooooooooooooooooooooaaaaaaaaaaaaaaaaalllllllllllllll llllllllllll!!!!!!!!!!!!!!!!!!

He barely had time to run off with his arm in the air before all the Grey Court players bundled him to the ground. 'Quality penalty, mate!' Wayne yelled from somewhere in the pile.

The final ten minutes felt like an hour. Declan's legs were aching but he kept running – mostly backwards into his own box to defend as Whitgift launched a flurry of late attacks. Declan won two headers, then saw defenders Will and Omar clear two more crosses.

As the ball rolled out for a throw-in, Declan tried to catch his breath. He signalled for Will to push up on the Whitgift left winger while closely marking their

Number 8, who he had been tracking all afternoon.

But there was no time for another attack. The referee blew the final whistle and Declan punched the air. He shook hands with the Whitgift players and then sat down on the pitch, taking it all in.

'Yes! Yes! Yes!' Omar shouted, jumping up and down.

'We did it, mate!' Sam screamed, racing over to Declan.

Declan and the rest of the boys enjoyed being the centre of attention at Grey Court over the next few weeks. It was another special moment to add to an ever-growing collection.

CHAPTER 9

JT

One of the biggest challenges at Chelsea was keeping pace with the other boys, as they all had growth spurts at different stages. Declan wasn't the biggest or the strongest, but he could do a little of everything. That made him one of the most versatile players in the academy – and this was proving to be both a good thing and a bad thing.

While his coaches loved that Declan could fill in at full back, centre back or anywhere in midfield, he found himself swapping positions on a weekly basis – and sometimes even within the same game. It could be unsettling for Declan. Did the coaches know what his best position was?

The academy training sessions had gone up a level over the past six months, in part because Chelsea legends often dropped by to assist the coaches or talk to the boys. John Terry was the most regular guest, and no-one was more excited than Declan, who had grown up with Terry as one of his football heroes.

'I've still got two "Terry 26" shirts in my wardrobe at home,' Declan told him proudly the first time they met.

Terry often jumped into the sessions to share his opinions and chatted with the boys during breaks. 'Just call me JT,' Terry said, after seeing Declan struggle with whether to call him John or Mr Terry or Coach.

He and JT quickly struck up a good relationship. Declan loved it when his hero would put on a bib and join in with their five-a-side games. Equally, he liked being able to fire questions at a Chelsea legend on everything from positioning to heading to healthy food.

'You've always got to be thinking a few steps ahead,' he explained to Declan at the end of one session. 'When you're dealing with a long ball, first you've got to make the judgement call on whether you can win the header. But in that same instant, if you won't get there, it's about the flick on and assessing how that could be dangerous.'

Declan was understanding more and more that quick decision-making could give him an advantage, and he found videos of some of JT's old games to learn from him.

Later that week, he was putting those lessons to good use. Reece James, another promising young player, burst forward on the right. Declan sprinted back, ready to defend a cross into the box. But, with a quick glance over his shoulder, he saw that there were no other players in the box and that Reece's only option was a cutback. Declan read it perfectly, waiting for Reece to commit to that pass and then swooping in to intercept it.

'Don't be afraid to get on the ball from the back,' JT frequently reminded him. 'You've got the touch and passing to do it. Just be confident. You can see the whole pitch from back there, whether you're in defence or deep in midfield.'

Declan nodded. With the ball at his feet, he knew he was one of the most reliable passers in the team. But the Chelsea coaches reminded him repeatedly about the physical side of the game. Declan wasn't small, but he was skinny. Suddenly, he was battling strikers and midfielders who had the strength to brush him aside.

'I know my body is still growing, but I just feel really awkward at the moment,' he told Mason as they jogged round the pitch one morning. 'I'm clumsier and I'm not running as smoothly. Hopefully it's just a phase.'

'Yeah, don't worry about it, mate,' Mason replied. 'We all have a few rough weeks here and there, and you were solid at training yesterday.'

It was true. He had played better the previous evening. He just needed to put the doubts aside and keep focusing on his game.

CHAPTER 10

CHAPTER 10

NOW
WHAT?

'Most of the time, being at the Chelsea academy is the coolest thing in the world,' Declan told Jordan one evening as they settled in to watch a Champions League game. 'Until we have to start thinking about our next contract...'

Declan left that thought unfinished and rested his head against the sofa cushion. No matter how well he felt he was playing, he knew there was always a chance that the Chelsea coaches could see things differently. There were so many good players at the academy – and Declan was often his own biggest critic after disappointing training sessions.

'Don't let that get to you,' Jordan said, passing his

brother a bowl of crisps. 'All you can do is give it your best in each practice. The rest is out of your hands.'

It was good advice but Declan found it challenging to follow through on. He loved life at the academy and it had become a second home. 'I just can't imagine playing for anyone else,' Declan added quietly. 'Chelsea is all I know.'

When decision day arrived for the Under-14s, Declan felt uneasy from the moment he woke up. He knew some of the other boys, including Mason, had received good news about their contracts. That made the waiting even more difficult.

He left his backpack and shoes by the front door when he got home from school and walked into the living room, where his dad was sitting on the sofa.

With one look at his dad's face, Declan had a bad feeling about what was coming.

'Come and sit down, Dec,' Sean said gently, pointing to a spot next to him on the sofa.

Declan felt his stomach drop like he was riding a roller coaster. His mouth was suddenly really dry.

'We got a call from Chelsea today,' Sean began.

'Look – there's no easy way to say this, Dec. They've decided to release you.'

Declan felt like he had been punched in the stomach. He had no words; he could hardly breathe.

'I'm sure it was a really tough decision,' his dad continued. 'Dec, I'm so sorry.'

Declan felt tears trickling down his cheeks as he buried his head in his dad's shoulder. He had imagined getting this kind of bad news a few times over the past week, but the reality was so much worse.

He sat with his dad for at least an hour, mostly watching TV in silence. 'I just wish I knew why,' Declan said suddenly. 'The Chelsea academy has been my whole life for the past seven years. What am I going to do now?'

'You'll get through this, son,' Sean said, giving Declan another hug. 'We're all here for you, and there's no rush to think about other plans. Today was a lot to digest and no-one expects you to just move on immediately.'

The phone rang again later that afternoon – and for a split second, Declan hoped it was someone at

Chelsea calling to say that there had been a mistake.

Then his dad appeared in the doorway of his bedroom, holding the phone. 'It's for you,' he said, sitting down on the bed next to Declan.

'Hello?' he said, hearing the sadness in his own voice.

'Dec, I heard the news and I had to call,' came the reply. It was JT.

Declan was stunned. He turned to his dad and covered the mouthpiece of the phone. 'It's JT!!!'

'These setbacks always feel like the end of the world,' JT said. 'I've been there too. I'm gutted for you and I know what the Chelsea academy meant to you, but you can't give up. Use this pain to work even harder and keep fighting. Even as the Chelsea door closes, be ready for other doors to open. You're a quality player and I still believe in you.'

Declan fought back more tears. Those words were just what he needed to hear. 'Thanks, JT,' he eventually replied, trying to sound calmer than he felt. 'It's all still a bit of a shock, but I'm going to bounce back.'

They talked for forty-five minutes and gradually Declan felt himself moving from heartbreak to strengthened determination. 'You've got my number, Dec,' JT added, as they said goodbye. 'Give me a buzz anytime if you want to chat things through.'

As it turned out, news travelled fast around the London academies. Declan had just finished talking to JT when the phone rang yet again. Sean answered it. Declan was still in disbelief that JT had taken the time to call him, but he suddenly started paying attention to his dad's conversation:

'Look, I'll talk to Declan… that sounds like a great opportunity, but this has been a very tough afternoon… I don't know if he's really up to this so soon… okay, tell me when and where, and I'll call back to confirm.'

Declan raised an eyebrow at his dad as the call ended. 'What was that about?'

Sean wasn't sure whether to look happy or sad. He had no idea how Declan would react to this. 'Hmmm, well, apparently the Fulham academy are big fans of yours,' he said. 'They heard about your contract not being renewed and wanted to express their interest in bringing you in – whether you want to join them for training tomorrow or wait for next week.'

Declan just stared at his dad. This was turning into the strangest, most emotional day of his life.

Following JT's advice and embracing new possibilities, Declan arrived at the Fulham academy, with his boot bag tucked under his arm. He knew it was going to be surreal after so many years at Chelsea – and it was – but he still dreamed of being a professional footballer. Maybe this would be his new path.

CHAPTER 11

A WARM WELCOME AT WEST HAM

'It's totally up to you,' Sean said gently, sitting down opposite Declan. 'Things are happening really fast and you don't need to rush your decisions.'

Declan nodded. Fulham had been in touch again after that first training session, but now West Ham were eager to welcome him for a trial. He took a deep breath. While the attention was flattering, this had felt like the most draining week of his life.

'I want to train with West Ham and see what that's like,' he said finally. 'Like JT said, the best thing I can do is try to move past the disappointment. I can't change that. So now let's see what's next.'

Teresa had joined Sean on the sofa. They looked

at each other and smiled at their son's maturity. 'We couldn't be prouder of the way you're handling this,' Teresa said. 'Just know that we're here for you no matter what you decide.'

On the drive to the West Ham academy, Declan wondered how he would feel to be the new boy after feeling so comfortable at Chelsea for so many years. But he was relieved to see some friendly faces.

'Welcome, Declan!' said a tall man in a West Ham jacket, shaking his hand warmly. 'I'm Tony Carr, the West Ham academy director. We know all about you from our battles with Chelsea. You'll probably recognise some of the boys.'

Even so, the coaches took care of quick introductions and, before Declan really had time to think about settling in with new teammates, he was into the flow of the session.

In the keep-ball sessions, the passes were flying around the circle, but Declan handled that with ease. When he needed to, he took two touches, but most of the time he flicked and steered first-time passes. He could see the West Ham coaches keeping a close eye on his group.

After running, passing and shooting drills, Declan smiled as he saw one of the coaches carrying mini goalposts onto a small pitch marked out with cones. Game time! The boys were split into three teams, and Declan ran over to get one of the yellow bibs when his name was called.

'Okay, you boys know the rules,' one of the coaches shouted. 'First goal wins. Winner stays on. Green against Red to start. Yellows, you're off.'

Declan jogged over to the touchline. In some ways, he was happy that the Yellows were sitting off first as he had a chance to get a refresher on his teammates' names.

'Alex, Gavin, Ricky and Luke,' Declan repeated, with a smile. 'Got it!'

As he walked over for another sip of water, he heard a cheer behind him. The Greens had scored and the Reds were trudging off.

'Yellows, you're on!' came the shout, accompanied by a blast of a whistle.

Declan ran over and got the ball out of the net, as he

was the nearest to it. He dribbled forward and, as one of the Greens closed him down, Declan flicked a pass to Gavin with the outside of his right foot.

Declan kept moving, faking a run forward and then dropping back again. 'Still here!' he shouted, as Gavin turned into trouble and had to hold off two defenders. He managed to poke a pass back to Declan, who instantly shimmied to his left and sent a through ball towards Ricky, who got there first but took a heavy touch out of play.

Ricky gave Declan a thumbs-up as he turned to run back. One of the coaches was clapping too.

After a few more clever passes, Declan felt a wave of excitement. While some of the boys were hunched over and panting, he was barely even sweating. He had shown he could pass, tackle and even organise the other players. All that was left to do was score a goal. He put that right with a run straight through the middle, knocking the ball past the last defender and racing ahead to tap in a simple finish.

Out of the corner of his eye, he saw a couple of the West Ham coaches smiling and clapping. 'That was beautiful, Declan!' one of them called.

By now, high praise for the newcomer must have reached Tony Carr, and Dave Hunt, head of academy recruitment, because they appeared on the touchline next to the coaches.

'So, is Declan looking as good as we expected?' Tony asked, as Declan fizzed a pass over to Ricky. 'He seems confident on the ball.'

'He's been a beast so far,' explained one of the coaches. 'He's got the vision and the technique to see the game two steps ahead.'

'I remember watching him at Chelsea a few times and I'm really surprised they released him,' Dave chimed in. 'I've always thought he'll be a classic Premier League centre back once his body fills out, and he could play in midfield too.'

'Well, it would just be nice to have him on our side this time!' Tony added. 'I'm sure we're not the only club hoping to swoop in here. Let's make our interest very clear and get connected with his family. They need to know that Declan will be happy at West Ham and that we're going to fully support his development.'

They all nodded in agreement.

As the weeks rolled on, Declan realised that he had found a second home at West Ham. He was making new friends and getting on really well with the coaches. When the time came to make it official as part of the academy, Declan had no hesitation in committing his future to West Ham.

CHAPTER 12

ANOTHER NERVOUS WAIT

'We're going to miss you!' Sam called as Declan said his goodbyes to his friends at Grey Court.

Declan's decision to sign with West Ham had sparked a flurry of changes that he himself was still digesting – and it wasn't just a new school. He was also in the process of packing a suitcase ready to move into a new home in Romford, arranged by West Ham so that he would be based closer for training and games.

He had promised himself that he would try to keep a positive attitude about everything. After all, these were all steps towards a career as a professional footballer – and Declan desperately wanted to make it to the top. But there were moments when it felt like his own life was being turned upside down.

Teresa sat down next to him one morning, sensing that he was bottling up some of his uncertainty. 'Listen, none of this is permanent,' she said. 'If you don't like the new digs, we'll come and get you and you'll be back in your room here in no time. The same goes for your new school. Remember, though, that your truest friendships at Grey Court will last well beyond this change.'

Before he knew it, Declan was into his new routine – waking up in a different bed in a new flat, putting on a new uniform at a new school, training with different players as he moved up the academy ladder at West Ham.

'Everyone has been amazing,' he told Mason on the phone one night. He was thankful to still be chatting with his old friend every week. 'West Ham and the school have done everything possible to make sure I'm comfortable. But I still feel homesick sometimes. I know I haven't moved far... I just, well, I miss that life.'

'I get it, mate,' Mason said. 'It's tough, especially with so much changing all at once. But you can do this. When things get difficult, you always manage to dig deep.'

Through it all, Declan could always count on another source of support and advice. Dennis, the club's minibus driver, became a regular fixture in Declan's life as they travelled back and forth from games and training together. Before long, Declan saw that he could trust Dennis with any questions or worries – and that made a huge difference at a time when so many things felt uncertain.

On the pitch, Declan was proving the West Ham coaches right for having faith in him. Whether they put him in central defence or central midfield, they knew what they were getting – a committed, tireless performance. For Steve Potts, manager of the Under-18s, Declan was quickly becoming one of the first names on the team sheet.

But some of the scars were still there after the pain of being released by Chelsea. As the next scholarship decision loomed for West Ham, Declan's stomach was in knots.

'I'm sure it's mainly because of what happened at

Chelsea, but I'm going to be uneasy until I have the scholarship contract in my hands to sign,' he told his dad when they met up for a weekend walk.

Familiar thoughts were flooding Declan's mind: Did I do enough in the last training session? Were they watching that misplaced pass or missed tackle?

'Don't overthink it,' Mason had told him during one of their regular text threads. But that was easier said than done.

His dad echoed that. 'Try not to think about it,' he suggested. 'You've got this far by buckling down, listening to the coaches and taking it one week at a time.'

'I just feel like I need one more big performance to settle it,' Declan added. 'That way, I'll make it impossible for them to think about releasing me.'

The following week, the West Ham Under-18s faced Fulham Under-18s in a London derby that had the extra layer for Declan of being the two teams he considered after leaving Chelsea. That night against Fulham, he was everywhere. Whether or not he really had anything to prove at this point, Declan was going to send a message.

He was so locked in on winning the midfield battle that the whole speed of the game slowed down for him. He made life miserable for the two Fulham central midfielders, stepping in repeatedly to intercept passes or steal the ball from them. Then, just as Steve often pushed for, Declan used the ball intelligently to keep possession, rather than chasing a wonder pass.

Back in his own box, he won a crunching tackle to deny Fulham a clear scoring chance. At the other end, he timed his run expertly and thumped a shot just wide. Declan often put Yaya Touré among the frontrunners on his list of favourite Premier League players, and tonight he was playing just like him.

In a back and forth second half, Declan escaped pressure near the edge of the penalty area and raced forward. After laying the ball off, he continued his run. As the ball was clipped back to him, he took one touch to steady himself and another to fizz a low cross into the six-yard box. Three players collided at the near post trying to clear the danger and the ball rebounded right to Dan, one of the West Ham midfielders, for the simplest of tap-ins.

Steve stayed on the touchline clapping until every West Ham player was off the pitch and on the way to the dressing room. Declan was the last to leave the pitch, and he got a handshake and a fist bump. 'You didn't put a foot wrong today,' Steve said as they walked together. 'That was the type of individual performance that I'd usually expect from older players on the brink of joining the first team, not from a sixteen-year-old.'

On Declan's way to the dressing room, he saw his dad standing by the edge of the pitch. Declan limped over, with aching legs, mud caked all over his kit and blood trickling from a cut on his knee. 'I think that was the big performance I was looking for,' he said grinning.

Sean didn't say a word. He just wrapped his son in a big hug.

CHAPTER 13

YOUNG HAMMER OF THE YEAR!

Soon, any worries about Declan's long-term future at West Ham were long gone, as he progressed faster than almost any other youngster in the academy. He was one of the first names in any discussion about players to put on the fast-track to the first team, with his coaches equally wowed by his talent and his work rate.

'Young players like him are so rare,' one of the academy coaches said at the end-of-year evaluation sessions. 'He just gets it. Tactically, he's so sharp and you only ever have to explain things once to him. He comes in every day with a great attitude and great confidence, but no ego.'

'Yeah, he's right up there at the top of the list of players I've coached, and we're so lucky he landed here,' Steve added. 'It's never easy to know how a fourteen-year-old will develop through the teenage years, but I'm sure that's one decision that Chelsea would love to do differently now.'

'So what's next for him?' asked Tony. This was one of the big questions of the day. Declan clearly needed to be challenged beyond academy games.

'Well, the first team has the US tour this summer and I really think Slaven and his coaching staff should take a look at him there,' Steve said, strongly believing that West Ham boss Slaven Bilić would love working with Declan. 'That's his call, obviously. But we could recommend it.'

There was agreement all around the table. 'A full season with the Under-23s would be good for getting him the game time he still needs, but I could see him fitting into the first team plans within the next two years,' Steve continued.

All the decisions came together quickly and just a week later Slaven tapped in Declan's number on his office phone.

Declan heard his ringtone from across the room and hurried over. He raised his eyebrows when he saw the call was coming from West Ham.

'Hello?' he said, taking a split-second to run through all the possible reasons for this call.

'Hi, Declan, it's Slaven Bilić,' said a deep, gravelly voice.

Declan's heart skipped a beat. This was not one of the possible reasons on his list. He dismissed the possibility of this being a prank, but needed to sit down as his legs became shaky.

'Er... hi,' he managed to reply, before recovering his confidence. 'As you can probably tell, I wasn't expecting to speak to you today!'

Slaven laughed. 'Well, there's no reason to worry. In fact, I'm hoping you'll have the opposite reaction. I've heard a lot of great things about your development in the academy and you've really stood out in the games I've watched.'

Declan opened his mouth to say something, but then stopped. He hadn't realised that Slaven had dropped in to see some of the youth team games.

'I want to go over two things with you. First, we want you to get regular minutes with the Under-23s this season... But I also want you to spend time with me and the first team.'

Declan's head was spinning, and he was glad that Slaven couldn't see the silly, smiling look on his face. He was sure he looked like a kid at a chocolate factory.

'The hard work starts even sooner than you're probably expecting,' Slaven continued. 'I've picked you in my squad for the US pre-season tour. It'll be a great chance for us to work closely with you, and for you to get a taste of life in the first team.'

Now Declan was really speechless.

'Take some time to digest all of this,' Slaven said, laughing. 'I've dropped a lot on you this morning! But the biggest takeaway is that we see great things ahead for you at West Ham if you continue to work hard and expand your game.'

'After this call, I'm going to think of so many things that I'll wish I'd said,' Declan said, laughing. 'I'm just kind of in shock... but happy shock.'

It would have been easy for Declan to reward himself for all his progress by spending a month on the beach. But he knew this was his chance to keep improving and stand out in the US. Yes, his inclusion in the squad was likely more about observing how the other first-teamers prepared themselves, but there could be opportunities to make a bigger impression and nudge Slaven to give him some game time.

Sure enough, Declan caught the eye in the first few training sessions. He seemed fitter and sharper than some of the other players and sparked loud cheers and applause with two inch-perfect passes.

The two-game tour began in Seattle, where Declan was named in the starting line-up. While the Seattle Sounders team were in the middle of their league season, the West Ham rust was very obvious. Declan was disappointed to lose 3–0, but it was hard to be too down on himself when he was gaining this extra experience, getting to know his teammates better and staying in nice hotels.

Declan came on as a substitute for almost thirty minutes in the second game in North Carolina, and he again felt like he had shown Slaven the qualities he brought to the team. As he settled into his seat for the long flight home, Declan was determined to use the past week as a springboard and take another step forward once the league season kicked off.

He did just that, working hard to improve his weaknesses and standing head and shoulders above the opposition while playing for the Under-23s.

As Declan put on his suit before the West Ham 2017 end-of-season awards dinner and did his best to fix his tie, he thought back to some of the year's highlights – the goal-saving tackles, the wonder strikes, the last-minute wins. It was fun to just hang out with his teammates for a night, without the last game or the next game to think about.

Towards the end of the event, Tony appeared on the stage to say a few words as academy director and give out some of the usual annual awards. One of the last awards was always Young Hammer of the Year – an award that had been won by some impressive names over the years.

'This is always a special one for me,' Tony

explained. 'We love to see our young players develop, both as footballers and as young men. This year's winner is a perfect example of that – a hard worker and a terrific teammate who consistently delivered big performances. The Young Hammer of the Year award goes to …Declan Rice.'

When Declan heard his name, he froze for a few seconds and then, with the other boys and parents cheering, he walked shakily up to the stage. Once there, he turned and saw the flashes of cameras and phones capturing the moment.

He was sure that his mum, dad and brothers were responsible for a lot of the noise. His girlfriend, Lauren, was also with them and he was sure that some of his success stemmed from how happy he was spending time with her. He caught sight of them all and waved.

This award was for all of them, as much as it was for him.

CHAPTER 14

DEBUT DELIGHT

The afternoon training session had been a long one, even with the season almost over. With the sun blazing, Declan took his time walking to the car. A quick shower had helped, but somehow he still felt sweaty... sweaty but as happy as he could remember.

A Rice family barbeque, planned for that evening, would be the perfect way to unwind and put his feet up – plus, the perfect moment to share some news!

He was the first one to arrive and he joined his dad outside, where the barbecue was already working overtime. 'Hey, Dec!' Sean called, turning over the burgers and sausages. 'Grab a drink.' He pointed to a little cooler under the table.

His mum appeared with a salad and burger buns, and they all sat down together to catch up on life. Within minutes, Jordan and Connor appeared and immediately tucked into the burgers.

Declan was bursting to make his big announcement, but he had wanted his brothers to be there. He finished his bite of burger and looked around the table.

'Have you thought about maybe getting away for a family trip this weekend?' he asked, trying to hide a smile.

His question was met with confused faces. 'What?' Jordan and Connor replied at the same time.

'Well, I've heard Burnley is lovely at this time of year,' Declan added, grinning.

After a brief pause, all four of them suddenly understood, and the confused looks turned into excited smiles. 'You're travelling with the first team again?' Sean said, jumping up out of his seat.

Declan laughed but held up his hand. 'Hang on, I'll probably just be sitting on the bench again. But it'll be a cool experience.'

Teresa let out a joyful scream. Connor and Jordan ran over for bear hugs that almost knocked Declan off his chair. His brothers starting singing 'I'm Forever Blowing Bubbles', the famous West Ham song, as Sean and Teresa came round for hugs of their own.

'You deserve this, son,' Sean said, his voice sounding a bit choked up. 'Of course we'll be there!'

Teresa smiled up at Declan. 'I'll tell everyone in the crowd that I'm your mum, even if you're on the bench for the whole game,' she said, laughing.

Declan rolled his eyes but hugged his mum tighter. 'I'm sure you will,' he replied, with a big grin.

Having closer links with the first team felt like a deserved reward for the season that he had put together as captain of the West Ham Under-23s. With Declan leading the way, they had clinched promotion, and the pace and physicality of the games seemed like a good rehearsal for life in the first team, where Declan was blown away by how talented every single player was.

Declan made sure he paid extra attention in the Sunday morning meeting as Slaven and the coaches walked through the tactics, the marking assignments at corners and what to expect from Burnley. He was used to some of this from the preparation at Under-23 level, but the detail in the first team scouting reports amazed him.

During the warm-up, Declan shut out all distractions. It helped that he wasn't the only youngster in the squad, plus he had got to know a few of the West Ham regulars at the evening meal at the hotel. James Collins and Aaron Cresswell had welcomed him over to their table and soon had him rolling around with laughter as they told funny story after funny story from their time at the club.

There was very little joking around now, though. Declan paired up with Aaron and they jogged, then sprinted, then jogged again as the coaches called out different instructions. The fans were starting to trickle into the stadium and Declan felt what he hoped was a healthy mix of nerves and excitement.

Back in the dressing room, Declan took a moment to admire the white 'RICE 41' shirt, which was hanging next to his boots and shin pads. Aaron appeared next to him. 'Don't worry, it's not a dream,' he said, grinning and patting Declan on the shoulder.

Declan took his place on the bench next to fellow academy players Moses Makasi, Domingos Quina and Dan Kemp, and tried not to fidget with all the energy surging through his body. After fifteen minutes, all the substitutes went down the steps to do some light running and stretching on the touchline. With one eye on the game going on just yards away, Declan rolled his neck from side to side and jumped up and down on the spot.

The minutes ticked by in the second half, with West Ham taking a 2–1 lead through an André Ayew goal. Maybe this wasn't going to be Declan's day after all. Slaven made one change with just over five minutes to go, and Declan remained in his West Ham tracksuit.

Then, with two minutes to go, Slaven began hurriedly gesturing for Declan to get ready. Declan didn't need to be told twice. In a flash, he piled his tracksuit trousers and warm-up top on his seat and walked over to one of the coaches, who flipped through a few tactical notes while they waited for the game to stop for the substitution. This was really happening. His West Ham debut! Declan felt a surge of pride as the reality set in. He was about to step onto the pitch as a Premier League footballer.

He willed the ball to go out for a goal kick or a throw-in. Finally, a West Ham clearance sailed into the stands. Edimilson Fernandes, the man being replaced, walked slowly towards the touchline, trying to use up as much time as possible. When he reached Declan, they high-fived and Declan ran onto the pitch, adding another highlight to an incredible season. Even with just a few thousand West Ham fans in the far corner of the stadium, he heard some cheers.

The crowd all around was a sea of purple and blue (the colours of both teams), so Declan had no chance of spotting his family, but he knew that somewhere in the stadium they would be on their feet cheering. He ran over to Manuel Lanzini with instructions on a slight tactical switch, then settled into a central midfield role next to him.

The number one priority was protecting the defence from late Burnley pressure, and he was immediately in the thick of the action. He slid in to win one 50-50 ball, then pinged a long pass over the top, forcing the Burnley defence into a panic, just as they wanted to be attacking at the other end.

At full-time, Declan shook hands with the Burnley players, then joined his teammates in applauding the travelling West Ham fans. Sure, he had only been on the pitch for a couple of minutes, but he couldn't stop smiling. This was the type of moment he had pictured so many times during his youth team years. Now, still just seventeen, he had been given his first taste of Premier League life.

Declan spotted his parents and brothers in the middle of the cheering West Ham fans. He waved and pumped his fist. His own joy, combined with their overflowing pride, brought on even more emotions. His mum blew kisses back – and Declan hoped none of his teammates had noticed.

Slaven was waiting for the players on the touchline and wrapped Declan in a big hug. 'Congratulations, Declan,' he said. 'Welcome to the Premier League! Something tells me this is the beginning of a very special career.'

Walking on air and feeling ten feet tall, Declan was one of the last players to make it back to the dressing room. He pushed open the door and, before he even had a chance to look up, water was flying at him from every direction. Aaron, James and André were at the front of a group of cheering players, spraying Declan with their water bottles.

They crowded round him.

'Nice one, Dec!' James said, hugging him.

'Big things ahead, buddy,' added Aaron, ruffling his hair and patting him on the shoulder.

Declan put his shirt aside, next to the clothes he had arrived in. As the kit man circled the dressing room, he stopped next to Declan and collected his shorts and socks, but didn't take the shirt. 'I'll leave that for you to take home,' he said, grinning. 'It's not every day that you make your Premier League debut.'

'Thanks,' Declan replied. He was already thinking about getting it framed for his parents' house.

But his work for the day wasn't done yet. The West Ham press team appeared and called a few of the

players for post-game interviews – André, Aaron...
and Declan.

Declan froze – not because he was shy, but just from
the shock of it. A reporter from West Ham TV introduced
himself, and suddenly Declan was staring into a camera
with a microphone just inches from his face.

'Ever since I started kicking a ball, it has always
been my ambition to play in the Premier League,
so my dream has come true and I'm delighted,' he
explained, when asked about his debut.

Declan had a chance for quick hugs and high-fives
with his family before scampering onto the team bus
for the long journey back down south. As he settled
into his seat and leaned back against the headrest,
he turned on his phone. It beeped and buzzed for
what felt like five straight minutes.

'Someone's popular!' shouted André, laughing.

'He's big-time now!' Aaron joined in.

Declan smiled. He had messages from all kinds
of people who had played a role in his development
over the years, both on and off the pitch.

As the bus pulled out of the stadium, his phone

buzzed again. It was a text from Mason. 'Proud of you, big man. We're going to take over the Premier League!'

CHAPTER 15

LEARNING FROM CLUB LEGENDS

The Premier League action came fast and furious – but Declan was willing to do whatever it took to survive. So far, he felt he had handled the step up in quality pretty well, but there was still so much to learn, even though he had been playing football all his life. At this level, it was just different. There was no other way to say it.

Luckily for Declan, he had Mark Noble in his corner.

'I've seen it all at West Ham over the years,' Mark explained. 'Plenty of talented young players have come through the youth ranks, and you're as good as any of them. Now it becomes about the mental side of the game as much as what you can do with the ball at your feet.'

'How do you mean?' Declan asked.

'Well, being a Premier League footballer brings a lot of pressure but also a lot of fame and money. The challenge is to keep football as your number one priority, even as your life changes. That sounds simple, but I've seen some fantastic players lose their way.'

Declan nodded. It made sense. He was already starting to hear about the perks that came with Premier League status.

'Just make sure you never lose the desire to keep improving,' Mark continued. 'The coaches here will push you, but you've got to be coachable and have your own drive to get better every day.'

Declan felt like he soaked up so much knowledge every time he played next to Mark in central midfield, even just on the training ground. He had often thought that he was a pretty vocal player – calling for the ball, shouting encouragement or instructions – but seeing Mark in action was a whole new level. The talking was constant, telling Declan who he was

marking and who he should stay close to, calling out
when to switch their marking assignments, where
the easiest next pass was, and when not to get fancy
under pressure.

His path to regular first-team action was made trickier
by some of the changes around him at West Ham. Early
in the 2017–18 season, Slaven was out and David
Moyes was in. Then David left that summer, with
Manuel Pellegrini taking over. Each time that Declan
felt he had proven himself, a new manager arrived.

While Declan was enjoying playing in midfield,
the West Ham coaches also saw him as a solid centre
back. Building on everything that he had learned
from JT, he continued to push himself to get better in
the air, stronger in the tackle and sharper at reading
dangerous attacks. To help with that, he spent a lot
of time with Matt Upson, another Premier League
defender that Declan had watched for years who was
now doing his coaching courses.

Part of the development process was analysing
each game and going back through the footage – 'film
study' as some of the coaches called it.

'Look at your positioning here,' Matt said, pausing the video clip and pointing. 'You're in the right place to cut out a through ball if the runner is coming from that side, but you're not seeing anything beyond your other shoulder.'

Matt stood up and showed Declan what he meant, setting his feet and hips so he could easily glance over his other shoulder without losing his balance.

Declan got up from his chair too, copying the positioning and nodding. 'Yeah, I see it,' he said.

'Your instincts are spot on,' Matt added. 'Most of the time you're spotting the danger before it even develops. But this might unlock another gear for you.'

It was a luxury that not every young player had. Declan knew that he was in a unique situation with JT, Mark and Matt standing by to share their knowledge, plus all the West Ham coaches. 'Sometimes it's as if I'm doing a test but I've got all the answers in my back pocket,' Declan told his parents when they came over for dinner later that week.

Teresa smiled. 'Well, it seems like you're on the way to getting top marks,' she said.

CHAPTER 16

AN EYE FOR GOAL

'Let's boss it out here today,' Mark said, as he and Declan jogged from cone to cone during the pre-game warm-up before a big London derby against Arsenal. 'Give them no time on the ball. No easy passes.'

Declan nodded, reaching over for a high-five. He had a focused look on his face as he thought back through the game plan that Manuel and the West Ham coaches had outlined that week. 'Let it rip if you get a sight of goal too,' he reminded Mark.

'Well, you're the nineteen-year-old, so you've got no excuse for not getting in the box,' Mark joked as they went through their final stretches before returning to the dressing room.

Fifteen minutes later, they were in the tunnel, and Declan felt the usual surge of nerves and excitement. The London Stadium was rocking and he looked anxiously down the line of players, silently urging the referee to lead the players out onto the pitch.

With Mark protecting the defence, Declan took every opportunity to push forward. When striker Marko Arnautović dropped deep, he sprinted into the space behind. As Felipe Anderson and Michail Antonio got into crossing positions on the wings, he tried to time his runs perfectly.

Just before half-time, Declan saw Felipe in space on the left and only one West Ham shirt in the penalty area. He jogged forward then burst into a sprint, leaving his marker in the dust. His eyes lit up as the cross curled towards him and he leapt to direct a header towards goal.

As he turned, there was the agony of seeing the ball fly just wide of the post. So close!

At half-time, Declan almost felt dizzy as Manuel paced around the dressing room, clapping and encouraging. 'More of the same!' he repeated over and over. Looking at Declan, he added: 'Keep making those runs. Even from the touchline, I can see the Arsenal defenders getting confused about who is tracking you.'

Declan bounded down the tunnel for the second half and set the example by charging around midfield to win the ball back. On the right, Felipe broke free and pushed the ball past the nearest defender. Declan instantly sensed an opportunity. He rushed into the box and screamed for the cutback.

Felipe's cross was cleared, but only as far as Samir, still just inside the penalty area. Declan took a few steps back. 'Square it, Samir!' he called, feeling like he had a better opening for a quick shot.

Samir gave him the perfect layoff, and Declan didn't hesitate. The pace of the ball set him up for a first-time shot and he caught it sweetly, whipping a shot into the top corner. *1–0!*

Goooooooooooooooooooooaaaaaaaaaaaaaaaaalllllllllllllll llllllllllll!!!!!!!!!!!!!!!!!!!

Declan couldn't have hit it any better. From the moment that the net rippled, everything was a blur.

He ran off towards the West Ham fans, sliding on his knees as Felipe and Mark piled on top of him.

It was his first West Ham goal – and this was a moment that he had pictured hundreds of times. The stadium had erupted and everywhere he looked there was a West Ham fan jumping or cheering.

'I told you!' Mark shouted over all the noise. 'When you get in the box, good things happen.'

Declan grinned, but he knew the job wasn't done yet. Arsenal threw more players forward for every corner or free kick, forcing Declan to listen carefully to the West Ham defenders on when to push up and when to track the run.

At the final whistle, all the West Ham players flocked over to Declan, fluffing up his hair and putting an arm around him. 'Are we sure he's really only nineteen?' Mark asked, smiling. 'You were in a different class today, Dec.'

CHAPTER 17

ALL=IN WITH
ENGLAND

As Declan's West Ham career took off, his progress at
international level wasn't far behind. He had already
played for the Republic of Ireland Under-17s and
showed the quality of his playing to such a high level
that he was picked for his debut for the senior team
in March 2018.

But then things got more complicated. Knowing
that Declan was born in London, England,
representatives confirmed their interest in bringing
him into their set-up instead. Faced with an incredibly
difficult decision, Declan took his time and talked
it through with his family, as well as with England
manager Gareth Southgate and Ireland head coach

Mick McCarthy.

'We know this is a huge decision for you, but we would have regretted it if we hadn't reached out,' Gareth told him. 'Take your time. Obviously, we think very highly of you, but I can't promise anything. Still, if you're eligible for England squads, it would give us a chance to take a closer look at you.'

The frenzy around England's run to the World Cup semi-finals back in 2018 had initially got Declan thinking about his options – and it was impossible not to get swept up in the buzz. He had watched England on TV with his friends and family at the World Cups in 2006, 2010 and 2014, sharing in the agony of those early exits. The 2018 scenes across England – even while Declan was taking it all in from afar in Dubai – had given him a shiver of excitement and a reminder of how amazing it would be to play at a major tournament. In truth, even as his career had blossomed, he just never envisioned being in demand like this at international level.

Whatever he decided, he knew there would be disappointed reactions from the fans and some angry backlash. In the end, after thinking it over for weeks, he made the choice to move forward with England.

Sitting down with the media, he explained his decision. 'I am a proud Englishman, having been born and raised in London,' he said. 'However, I am just as proud of my family's Irish heritage and my affinity and connection with the country. I have equal respect and love for both England and Ireland and therefore the national team I choose to represent is not a clear-cut, simple selection. Particularly not for a young lad who never dreamed of being in this position.'

Predictably, there were some harsh comments online and on TV about Declan's decision, but he blocked out the noise and focused on making the most of whatever international opportunities came his way with England.

'There are no guarantees with England,' Declan admitted when chatting again with his parents. 'I totally get that. But I just think I'll wonder "what if" for the rest of my life if I don't give myself a shot at getting into the squad.'

The next step was submitting a formal request to

FIFA to switch nationalities. Declan completed the paperwork and then sat back to wait. If it all went smoothly, he could even be eligible for selection for England's next game.

In the meantime, Declan felt freer to produce his best form for West Ham without the pressure to make a decision hanging over his head. He was still learning every day in training and battling to keep up with all the Premier League stars, but he was clearly doing something right. Manuel picked him to start thirty-four of the team's thirty-eight league games during the 2018–19 season. Declan proudly collected his third consecutive Young Hammer of the Year award as further recognition of how quickly he had settled into the first team.

His football journey had taken some interesting turns already, and Declan had a feeling that this latest choice would only add to the excitement.

CHAPTER 18

THREE LIONS ON THE SHIRT

It was a moment that Declan would never forget – and another reason he was glad he always kept his phone by his side.

'You'll be in the England squad announced later today. Congratulations, Declan, we're excited to work with you.'

Those special words from England manager Gareth Southgate played on repeat in Declan's head as he prepared to take the next step in his young career. After getting the call from Gareth, he had immediately shared the news with his family and, now that the squad had been announced, a wave of messages flooded his phone.

All the excitement and congratulations were nice, but Declan quickly shifted his focus to making a strong first impression. He didn't just want to be 'happy to be there'; he wanted to show that he could bring his outstanding West Ham form onto the international stage.

The first of the two games during the international break was at Wembley against the Czech Republic, followed by a trip to Montenegro.

Though Declan felt some nerves as he arrived at the England camp, it certainly helped that there were some familiar faces. Looking around the room, he saw other youngsters like Ruben Loftus-Cheek and Trent Alexander-Arnold. They must be feeling the same mix of emotions, he thought.

The veterans in the squad gave him a warm welcome. Declan arrived early for one of the team meetings and wasn't sure where to sit. Harry Kane spotted him, waved him over and pointed to the chair next to him.

'Welcome to the England squad, Declan,' he said. 'I've watched you a lot this season and you've been brilliant.'

Looking back on the first few days with the England squad, Declan really felt like his game had gone up another level.

'That's what happens when you're taking on the best players in the country every day,' his brother Connor told him. 'You have to raise your game to keep pace with them.'

Gareth named his team to face the Czechs, and Declan was among the substitutes. 'Stay ready,' the coaches noted, hinting at a possible role off the bench in the second half.

Getting off the bus at Wembley and walking around the pitch pre-game, Declan couldn't stop smiling. He was living out his dream – and the dreams of young boys all over the country. The pitch felt like a big green carpet, and he had to drag himself back to the dressing room in the end, as he would have happily continued walking around for another hour.

As the starting eleven high-fived and headed for the tunnel, Declan couldn't help but feel envious. Being in the squad was an incredible thrill, but walking out onto the pitch to soak up the cheers and sing the national anthem was... well, hopefully something he would experience as part of the starting line-up in the years ahead.

There was an early injury scare for England as midfielder Eric Dier limped off. For a moment, Declan allowed himself to wonder whether he would be brought on, but Gareth opted for Ross Barkley. England dominated the Czech Republic from the start, and Declan jumped up to celebrate the first-half goals.

As they extended the lead in the second half, Declan started to wonder if some of the substitutes might get a chance in the final few minutes with the win secured. Maybe. He jogged towards the corner flag, waved to the fans, turned and walked back, stopping to stretch every few paces.

He was about to go up the steps back to his seat, when Gareth signalled for him to come over. Declan froze for a second, then walked pitchside to where his manager was standing.

Gareth and assistant Steve Holland huddled around him. 'Alright, Declan, we'll be bringing you on in a few minutes to replace Dele Alli,' Gareth said.

'You'll slot in at the base of the midfield. Just play your natural game. Show for the ball and shield the back four.'

Declan nodded to show he was paying attention, but part of his brain was just screaming, 'Wow!!!' He took off his bib and warm-up top, then pulled up his socks, slotted in his shin pads and took a deep breath. Around the country, he knew there would be shrieks of excitement from all those people who had played a part in Declan's journey.

The assistant referee raised his electronic board. Declan took a deep breath and could feel his heart hammering in his chest. He waited patiently for Dele to walk over, then bounded onto the pitch. Jordan Henderson came over to give Declan a quick high-five and wish him luck.

The nerves disappeared after his first few touches, and there was less pressure with England already 3–0 up. He just tried to soak it all in. England scored twice more, and Declan raced over to celebrate in front of the fans.

'Well done today, Declan,' Gareth said as they walked

back down the tunnel together at the end of the game. 'You looked right at home in an England shirt.'

Declan beamed. 'Thanks, boss,' he replied. 'I loved every minute of it.'

Now he had given Gareth some real selection headaches for the next game. There was a midfield role up for grabs with Eric out injured – had Declan done enough to snatch it?

On the Sunday afternoon, Declan joined the rest of the squad for a team meeting to discuss the plans for the next few days before the flight to Montenegro. 'That was a terrific performance yesterday,' Gareth said once all the players were sitting down. 'We're going to take things easy here today and then ramp up the preparation for Wednesday. You'll find all the information in the packs that Steve is handing out.'

At the end of the meeting, the players began to file out of the room and head back to their rooms. Declan was at the back of the line and was already busy flipping through the info pack. He looked up as he got to the door and saw Gareth waving him over.

After taking a second to make sure it was definitely

him that Gareth was calling, Declan walked across the room.

'How are you feeling?' Gareth asked, patting Declan on the shoulder. 'Lots of emotions yesterday, I'm sure!'

'I feel great,' Declan replied. 'I got a good night's sleep once I'd replied to all the messages from friends and family. That took a while!'

Gareth laughed. 'Well, I wanted to get a quick word with you now with Montenegro in mind. Eric is going to have to miss Wednesday's game and you'll be starting in his place.'

Declan smiled. 'I can't even pretend to play it cool,' he said. 'That's amazing news, boss. I'll be ready.'

'We know you will be,' Gareth said, offering Declan a handshake. 'You've earned this. We've been really impressed with your ability and your attitude this week. Just keep this to yourself for now. I wanted to give you a little extra time to process it all – but we'll be announcing it to the squad tomorrow.'

After thanking Gareth again, Declan tried to walk normally as he moved towards the nearest hotel lift. But he was sure he was actually skipping or floating.

What a feeling!

Boosted by his strong cameo and the prospect of a full debut in Montenegro, Declan was on fire in training over the next few days. He had that little bit of extra confidence to try passes and shots that he would have hesitated to attempt the previous week. In the mini-games, he was a blur – intercepting passes, playing slick one-twos and creating an extra yard to get on the ball.

Sitting on his bed the night before the game, he knew he would struggle to fall asleep with such a huge day ahead, so he watched some TV and listened to music to relax. Nothing could have prepared him for the thrill of walking onto the pitch for his full England debut, hearing the national anthem and seeing the section of travelling fans making as much noise as they could.

Against Montenegro, Declan felt less nervous than in his substitute role against the Czechs. There was something reassuring about starting the game and being into the flow of the action straightaway. When the opposition took a shock lead, the stadium quickly became louder and more hostile. But Declan didn't let any of that get to him. He just played his natural game, picking up loose balls in midfield and feeding passes to Raheem Sterling and Ross Barkley, who both seemed to be escaping their markers with ease.

England powered back to win 5–1, with Declan playing a sharp pass to start the move for the third goal.

Declan had made his mark and quickly became an England regular. After a big 4–0 win away to Kosovo, where he was again in the starting line-up, Declan was still riding the wave of excitement at international level. His brothers had just been telling him how much the country was rallying behind this England team and how many younger fans seemed to be wearing England shirts these days – and not just shirts for their favourite club team.

It got Declan thinking about Grey Court and something he had been meaning to do for a while. He had stayed in touch with Mr Willmore over the years, but he was overdue for a visit to his old school.

Back at home, Declan messaged Mr Willmore

about this idea and some possible days and times that could work for the next week. He got an enthusiastic thumbs-up from Mr Willmore and the school headmaster – and, before he knew it, he was back on some very familiar streets.

Walking into Grey Court again was a special feeling, and lots of good memories resurfaced for Declan. There had been changes at the school since his days there, but the place still mainly looked the same.

As soon as Declan walked into the playground, the kids swarmed around him with a mix of shock and excitement. They crowded in for selfies and autographs. 'You're a legend!' one boy shouted. 'We love you, Declan!' screamed a group of girls.

A couple of times, Mr Willmore looked over apologetically and seemed like he was going to come across to rescue him. But Declan smiled and held up his hand to let Mr Willmore know that he was fine and there was no need to cut things short. He stayed in the playground until he had posed for every last photo and signed every last autograph.

'They'll never forget this!' Mr Willmore said

happily as he led Declan off to meet with a few of the other teachers that he would remember from his time at Grey Court. Then Declan headed to the main assembly hall for a question-and-answer session. The kids had a chance to raise their hand and ask him anything. He fielded questions on a range of topics, from life in the England squad, to his favourite West Ham teammates, to his dream car.

As Declan was finally saying his goodbyes and promising to plan another visit soon, Mr Willmore was still apologising for taking up so much of his time. 'I really thought it would just be an hour or so, Declan,' he said. 'I know this isn't the most restful way to spend your time off.'

'Honestly, I loved it,' Declan said, smiling. 'Everything has happened so fast for me since I left Grey Court. Coming back here helps me stay connected to my childhood.'

'Well, we're all incredibly proud of what you've achieved so far and the example you set for younger players. We can't wait to watch the next phase of your career.'

Declan gave Mr Willmore a hug. 'Don't forget, a lot of my character was formed here,' he said. 'I'm being asked to do more and more as a leader and as a player now, and it makes me even more thankful for what I learned from you while playing for the school team.'

CHAPTER 19

A HOLIDAY SCARE

'It feels good to have this offseason break, away from the pressure and the media spotlight,' Declan admitted to Mason as they enjoyed the summer sunshine in Dubai.

Declan and his girlfriend Lauren had planned the holiday months ago and, by chance, Mason and his girlfriend were there at the same time. There was no chance that the two friends were going to miss out on catching up together. Lauren had rolled her eyes and laughed when she heard – of course this was happening!

'Yeah, it's starting to get harder to go out without being photographed these days,' Mason said. 'Did

you ever think we'd get to this point when we were
teaming up at Chelsea?!'

'It's wild,' Declan agreed. 'I'm not sure I'll ever get
used to the photographers following us around.'

'It's so nice to see the two "brothers" reunited,'
Lauren joked, joining them. 'And don't worry... I'll
make sure fame doesn't go to your heads.'

Sipping drinks and tucking into a plate of delicious
snacks, Declan could have no complaints. It was the
kind of moment where he wished he could freeze
time and just savour it.

It had been a long day in the sun after a fun party
the night before. Declan yawned and decided to get
out of the heat. He went inside and lay down on the
sofa. Within minutes, he was fast asleep.

When Mason came in for some water thirty minutes
later, he immediately heard the snores coming from
the other room – and he sensed a golden opportunity.

Taking his phone out of his pocket, he started
filming as he walked towards the sofa where Declan
was sleeping. Mason tiptoed across the carpet and
then, when he was just a few steps away, started

shouting loudly.

Declan's eyes opened with a start, and he let out two piercing screams, with panic all over his face. What had happened? Where was he? Who was yelling?

Mason collapsed with laughter, but not before he had checked to make sure everything was captured on video. 'That's gold!' he said to himself as he watched the video on loop.

Once Declan was awake enough to understand what had happened, he had to laugh too. 'Fair play, Mase,' he said. 'That was amazing. But, just know, I'll get you back when you least expect it!' He unleashed his best evil laugh.

Mason posted the video online and before long it had gone viral, with millions of views and a long string of comments.

'Well, when I was talking about your fame earlier, this isn't really what I had in mind!' Lauren called out, watching the video again on her phone and grinning as the number of views continued to climb.

'If people didn't know you before, they will now!' Mason added. 'You're the screaming guy!'

Declan could already picture how much fun his West Ham teammates would have with this video once preseason arrived.

'So much for a quiet break away from the spotlight!' Declan said, throwing a cushion at Mason.

CHAPTER 20

WEARING THE ARMBAND FOR WEST HAM

'I'm sure you don't want to talk about the R-word, but what's the mood like in the dressing room?' Jordan asked as he, Connor and Declan chatted away on one of their regular video calls. The 2019–20 season was off to a rough start for West Ham.

'Well, I feel like there's no point in shying away from it,' Declan replied. 'We are in a relegation battle, and we've got to embrace that challenge.'

'These are the moments when you really shine, Dec,' Jordan said, trying to lift his brother's mood. 'You'll figure it out.'

'Well, on that topic, I have some news to update you on,' Declan added. 'With Mark battling injuries, that leaves not just a gap to fill in midfield but also as captain. So, Manuel called me into his office yesterday.'

He paused just for the fun of building suspense.

'And...?' Connor asked. 'What did he say?'

'He wants me to be ready to step in as captain if Mark has to miss any games,' Declan said, smiling proudly.

'Whoa!' Connor replied, his mouth wide open. 'How do you feel about doing that when you're still so young?'

'Mostly I'm proud, really. There's extra pressure, for sure, but I think I can help bring everyone together to turn things around.'

Declan could still hear Manuel's words echoing from their meeting. 'Ever since you broke into the first team, we've seen you as a future leader and a future star,' his boss had explained. 'I know we're throwing you right into this, but we think you're the right choice to captain the team when Mark isn't available.'

While Declan recalled agreeing and feeling the excitement bubble up, the rest of the conversation was a bit of a blur. But he knew that things would be a little different now when the squad returned to the training ground. There was no denying that a twenty-year-old stand-in captain was unusual in a squad with plenty of senior players.

Before he knew it, that responsibility was real. Mark was ruled out for a game against Leicester in November – and Declan was going to be taking over the armband.

'Oi, skipper!' came a voice from across the cafeteria. Declan turned to see Mark walking over in a West Ham tracksuit with a big grin on his face. 'How are you feeling?' he asked.

The nice thing about Declan's friendship with Mark was that he could be honest with him. 'I'm a bit more nervous than I expected,' Declan said. 'It's a big ask to step into your shoes for the next few games and I just don't want to let anyone down.'

'Even though you're probably young enough to be my son, the lads really look up to you,' Mark said reassuringly. 'We all know you're built for this.'

Declan smiled. 'Any words of wisdom for me?'

'Be authentic and be yourself,' Mark replied

instantly. 'That's what the lads will respond to.'

Before he knew it, Declan was walking into the home dressing room to find the usual 'Rice 41' shirt hanging at his locker plus a new addition next to his boots – a captain's armband.

He had thought a lot about Mark's advice. It wasn't his style to stand up in front of the whole team and give a big speech, so he wasn't going to try to fake it. Instead, he worked his way around the dressing room, giving fist bumps and words of encouragement to each of the players.

Making his way towards the tunnel, Declan had to remember that he needed to be at the front of the line now. He smiled at the little girl who had been brought over to walk onto the pitch with him. 'Are you excited?' he asked.

The girl was very shy but eventually nodded.

'I'll let you in on a little secret,' Declan said. 'This is all kind of new to me too. Do you think we can help each other to make it less scary?'

The girl smiled and nodded again, just as the referee gave the signal and led the teams out onto the pitch.

The referee blew the whistle for the coin toss and Declan trotted over, getting flashbacks once again to his days captaining the Under-23s.

He won the toss and jogged back to join his teammates. 'We're off to a good start, lads,' he said, smiling. 'Tails never fails.'

But not much else went right for West Ham that afternoon, as their struggles deepened with a 2–1 loss. Boos rang out around the stadium, and Manuel was sacked as manager shortly after the game.

As Declan sat in a quiet dressing room, he knew there were going to be some really difficult days ahead.

CHAPTER 21

2019–20: FIGHTING FOR PREMIER LEAGUE SURVIVAL

As it turned out, the weeks and months ahead were even more difficult than Declan had imagined. While David Moyes's return had boosted the mood in the squad, West Ham were still near the bottom of the table, sitting in seventeenth place – one spot outside the drop zone.

Then, the season was paused. The past few months had brought the kind of unique situations that no Premier League footballer was ever prepared for. With a global health crisis bringing the season to a screeching halt, Declan had found himself with a lot of unexpected free time, but with nowhere to go.

Now the players were preparing for the season

to get going again, having had no chance to train together with the coronavirus pandemic health risks. Returning with fresher legs for the fight ahead, it was still an odd feeling to be gearing up for club games in June and July.

'We just want to get back on the pitch and give people something to smile about again,' Declan said. 'The pressure gets pretty overwhelming if we look too far ahead. So, as boring as this probably seems, we're taking it one game at a time.'

Connor laughed. 'You sound like a true West Ham spokesperson!' he said.

Mark was able to fight through the pain and play in the first two games after the long break, but as the third game approached, at home to Chelsea, he knew he needed to give himself more recovery time. Declan would be captaining the team again.

'We really need this one,' Declan told Jordan, as he called him from the car on the way to the stadium.

'Make sure you get stuck into Mase then,' Jordan said, laughing. 'Remember, he'll know all your tricks.'

The players walked down the tunnel. An empty

stadium greeted them, with fans not yet allowed to return to the stands given all the health concerns.

'We don't have the fans today, so we've got to bring the noise ourselves,' Declan told his teammates as they huddled on the pitch before kick-off. 'Get stuck in, keep talking and stay cool. If we do all that, the three points are ours.'

He clapped loudly and high-fived Aaron and Michail, then readjusted the armband on his sleeve.

West Ham matched Chelsea in the first half, with Declan leading the tireless pressure in midfield. He was rushing over to celebrate what he thought was the first goal when Tomáš Souček bundled the ball over the line, but it was overturned for offside. Minutes later, Chelsea won a penalty and took a 1–0 lead.

It would have been easy for West Ham to drop their heads and have that sinking feeling again. But Declan refused to think that way. He just ran harder and further, setting an example for his teammates to follow. In first-half stoppage time, Tomáš headed in an equaliser.

Now they had some momentum. Just after half-
time, Declan pushed forward to join an attack, feeding
the ball into Michail's feet. The ball then found Jarrod
Bowen on the right and his cross was perfect for
Michail to slide the ball home. *2–1!*

Chelsea pulled level with a well-placed free kick,
but Declan dug deep for an extra gear. Mason had
come on as a substitute and Declan clattered into him
to win one loose ball. 'Sorry, mate,' he said, as Mason
hit the turf.

In the final minutes, Declan got to a loose ball first
and hooked a clearance forward to Michail to start
a speedy counter-attack. Michail laid the ball off to
Pablo Fornals, got it back and then released substitute
Andriy Yarmolenko on the right. Andriy had the
freshest legs on the pitch and he raced forward to curl
the winning goal into the bottom corner.

'Come on!!!' Declan screamed, as the celebrations
echoed around the empty stadium. What a win!

Back in the dressing room, the mood was hopeful
again. 'Terrific performance, lads,' David said, clapping
and looking as relieved as the players felt. 'That gives

us a little breathing room above the relegation zone, but we've got to bring this same energy and effort for the final six games. If you play like you did today, we'll be in great shape.'

But a 2–2 draw with Newcastle and a 1–0 loss to Burnley cranked up the pressure once again. 'These next two games are huge,' Declan said to Aaron as they jogged around the pitch at the start of a midweek training session.

'Yeah, if we can get at least four points from those games, I'll probably be able to sleep a little better,' Aaron replied.

Mark was back for the trip to Norwich, and together they dominated in midfield. Michail scored all four goals in a 4–0 win, but Declan and Mark had their fingerprints all over the game.

'Now we've got to take care of business at home to Watford,' Declan told his parents on the phone, brushing off the congratulations as West Ham still weren't out of danger. 'If we win that, we're almost safe.'

Maybe it was a good night's sleep, maybe it was the carry-over from thumping Norwich, but Declan felt great as he arrived at the stadium. That continued throughout the warm-up with every touch of the ball. He knew the stakes were high today, but he tended to produce his best performances when the lights were brightest.

Michail kept his red-hot form going with a clinical early finish, settling some of the nerves. Tomáš doubled the lead by the ten-minute mark as Declan began to dream about Premier League survival.

Still, there were enough scares at the other end to keep the pressure on. 'Stay switched on!' he reminded the back four after one Watford counter-attack. We need a third goal, he thought to himself.

As Mark got into space down the left wing, Declan moved forward and created room for a pass. Mark clipped the ball back to him and Declan had already taken a glance to see that there was no Watford player within five yards of him. He took one decisive touch to cut inside and get the ball onto his right foot, then decided to try his luck.

Declan pulled back his right foot and unleashed a rocket shot towards the far corner. Just like in the warm-up, he struck it sweetly and looked up to see it arrowing towards the goal. The Watford goalkeeper barely moved as the shot whistled past him into the net. *3–0!*

Goooooooooooooooooooooaaaaaaaaaaaaaaaaaalllllllllllllllllllllllllllll!!!!!!!!!!!!!!!!!!!!!!!

With his biggest smile of the season, Declan raced off to celebrate, with his arms out, and wrapped David in a joyful hug on the touchline. The relegation fears were almost history.

Watford pulled one goal back, but West Ham stayed in control. As the final whistle sounded, the emotions came pouring out. Declan dragged his aching body towards his teammates. Mark grabbed him and Aaron in an exhausted hug, and the rest of the team soon appeared around them. This group had dealt with relegation worries for months – made even longer by the enforced mid-season break – and now they could finally relax. Mathematically, they still needed a point from their last two games, but their goal difference made it all but impossible to be caught now.

The dressing room scene was a special one. With

laughter and excited chatter all around, Declan slumped down at his locker, incredibly tired but incredibly happy.

To provide a perfect ending to this topsy-turvy year, Declan walked away with the Hammer of the Year award for the first time. As he clutched the trophy, he took a moment to think back through his years at West Ham and his rise to becoming one of the club's most important players.

CHAPTER 22

2020–21: EXCEEDING EXPECTATIONS

A new season brought a welcome fresh start for Declan and his teammates, even with a shorter-than-normal summer break.

'I never want to go through that kind of relegation battle again,' Declan said as he and Aaron brought their plates of food over to a table in the corner of the cafeteria during the preseason.

'With the talent out there in the training sessions this week, we really shouldn't have any worries like that this year,' Aaron replied.

Declan nodded as he ploughed through a plate of chicken and pasta. 'On our day, we can compete against anyone.'

He knew the main ingredients were there for a successful 2020–21 campaign. Michail had developed into a reliable Premier League striker, while Jarrod was a playmaker capable of tying defences in knots. He, Tomáš and Mark could dominate midfield, and Aaron and Angelo Ogbonna were dominant at the back. Keeper Łukasz Fabiański had come to the rescue countless times last season and had given everyone confidence.

'We found a rhythm at the end of last season,' Declan added. 'Hopefully, with just a short summer break, that form carries over to this season.'

David was clearly thinking along the same lines. 'Let's continue where we left off,' he told the West Ham players in one of their preseason meetings. 'I see we're already being written off by a lot of people. But that's fine. We have a chance to shock the league with a big bounce-back year.'

Two losses to start the season didn't change the positive mood in the dressing room, and Declan and his teammates were soon ripping through teams that had finished well above them in the table last year.

But a disastrous first half against Tottenham left Declan shaking his head as he walked off the pitch. Trailing 3–0, West Ham had been outclassed. He knew, though, that part of his job as captain was to rally the team in these moments. He and David delivered the same message: it's not over yet.

Declan set the tone at the start of the second half with two thundering tackles. West Ham looked livelier. But, with eight minutes to go, it was still 3–0.

'Keep pressing, lads!' Declan called. 'Let's get one back!'

Aaron swung in a free kick and Fabián Valbuena thumped a header into the bottom corner. 3–1. Declan raced to get the ball and hurry back to the halfway line. Three minutes later, a low shot was deflected in by a Tottenham defender for an own goal. *3–2!*

'Come on!' Declan shouted, with the yells echoing around the empty stadium.

He jogged into the box for another free kick deep in injury time. Aaron gave the signal and Declan made the near post run. He leapt as high as his tired legs would lift him, but the ball went a fraction too high.

As Declan was still holding his head in disappointment about how close he was to getting a flick, the ball rebounded out to Manuel. With nothing to lose this late in the game, Manuel smashed a first-time shot with the outside of his right foot. Declan turned to see it arrow into the top corner via the underside of the bar. 3–3!

'Unbelievable!' Declan screamed, chasing Manuel over to the far corner.

Back in the dressing room, it was mayhem, with players cheering and music pumped up to maximum volume. 'We never quit!' Declan shouted, hugging Aaron and Manuel. 'What a game!'

Declan's whirlwind season continued when he joined up with his England teammates to face Iceland. He was again playing a deeper role, but he had instructions to get into the box for free kicks and corners.

When Phil Foden lined up a free kick on the left, Declan made another near post run, just like he had against Tottenham. This time, he saw the ball curling right onto his head. All he had to do was direct it down into the corner. Declan timed it perfectly.

With a little glance off his head, the ball flew into the net. *1–0!*

Goooooooooooooooooooaaaaaaaaaaaaaaaalllllllllllllll lllllllllllll!!!!!!!!!!!!!!!!!!!!

His first goal for England! It seemed like one big celebration after another at the moment for Declan. He carried that momentum into the rest of the season as West Ham battled to stay in the race for European football. Just as Declan had always believed, the Hammers could match even the likes of Manchester City and Liverpool on their day.

Heading into the final day of the season, West Ham needed a win to be sure of qualifying for the Europa League. 'We've come too far to give it away now,' Declan told his teammates as they all put on their shirts, taped their ankles and prepared to leave the dressing room.

Pablo settled the nerves with two first-half goals, then Declan put the icing on the cake. Sprinting onto a long ball, he was too quick for the chasing defenders. He took his time, then powered a shot into the net. *3–0!*

*Goooooooooooooooooooaaaaaaaaaaaaaaaaalllllllllllll
lllllllllllll!!!!!!!!!!!!!!!!!!!!!!!!*

The fans jumped around wildly in the stands, and
Declan and his teammates soaked in the applause.
He couldn't have imagined a better ending to this
memorable season, or a better way to kick-start a
big summer.

CHAPTER 23

EURO HIGHS AND LOWS

'It's finally here!' Declan said excitedly when he called his parents from England's hotel base for the Euro 2020 tournament, which had been delayed to the summer of 2021 due to the coronavirus pandemic.

'Make it worth the wait!' they both replied.

Since making his debut in 2019, Declan's consistent performances for West Ham had made him a regular in Gareth's England squads. It had been a long season but joining up with the other England lads provided an extra spark of energy.

'We know we're dealing with high expectations this time around,' Gareth explained. 'Reaching the semi-finals at the World Cup was a huge step forward for us, no question. Take confidence from that, but we'll have to be even better to win this tournament.'

Of course, being in the England squad with Mason for a major tournament was beyond their wildest childhood dreams. They sat together for lunch the day before England's first group game at Wembley, with lots on their minds.

'Croatia, Czech Republic and Scotland,' Declan said, rattling off the teams in England's group. 'What do you reckon, Mase?'

'It could be worse,' Mason replied. 'But no team that reaches the tournament is going to be a pushover. Hopefully, the fans will give us an extra boost.'

Croatia, likely to be the toughest group stage opponent, were up first for England. All week, Declan had been working with Mason and Kalvin Phillips to get the right chemistry for a three-man midfield. Mason would be playing a little higher up the pitch, with Declan and Kalvin taking charge in front of the back four. The biggest threat would come from Luka Modrić – and Declan expected to spend a lot of the afternoon shadowing the Real Madrid star.

'If we shut him down, we take a big step towards shutting Croatia down,' Declan said to Lauren, who was counting the days to that first game too.

Declan did just that, helping England bag a 1–0 win with a typical all-action performance. A disappointing 0–0 draw followed against Scotland, then a narrow victory over the Czech Republic. The mood in the dressing room was a strange mix of happiness at reaching the knockout rounds, but frustration that things weren't clicking yet on the pitch.

'Defensively, we've looked solid, but we can play a lot better going forward,' he told Connor on the phone after beating the Czech Republic. 'And we'll have to against Germany in the next round.'

Declan had been excited for all of the group games, but the build-up to a knockout round game against Germany at Wembley was a whole new level of anticipation. 'The stakes will be high,' he said to Mason during one training session. 'If we win, we'll be heroes. If we lose, well… we probably shouldn't turn on the TV for a while.'

Gareth was expecting a physical battle against the

Germans – and that suited Declan just fine.

Standing in the tunnel and hearing the roar of the crowd, Declan felt the hairs on his arms and on the back of his neck stand on end. He looked down at the England badge on his shirt and smiled, nodding to himself. 'Let's go!' he said to himself quietly, as the players began the walk out onto the pitch.

The next ninety minutes were everything Declan expected from a game against such long-standing rivals. It was physical and bruising, but he was never one to shy away from a tackle. He prowled around midfield, tracking runs and snapping in to break up attacks. For almost seventy-five minutes, it was a stalemate. Then Declan watched as Luke crossed from the left and Raheem steered a first-time shot into the net.

Wembley erupted. Declan punched the air and raced over to jump on the pile of celebrating teammates. These were the kinds of moments he had pictured as a kid – and now he was right in the middle of them! Harry added a second goal right at the end and England were into the quarter-finals.

Gareth gave the players some freedom to savour the historic afternoon, but it was all business the next day, with a match-up against the Ukraine to prepare for. For the first time in the tournament, Declan and his teammates would be leaving Wembley. 'We've just got to find a way to win in Rome,' he said to Mason, while they were waiting for the flight to Italy. 'Then we get the semi-final and final at Wembley.'

On paper, the quarter-final was a mismatch, but Declan had been an England fan for long enough to remember the team slipping up on other banana skins at prior tournaments. Harry Kane got them off to a dream start, with a sharp finish from Raheem's pass, and then England piled forward in search of some knockout blows. Declan's eyes lit up when the ball bounced invitingly in front of him, but his powerful shot was well saved by the Ukraine keeper.

'The second goal is coming,' Declan said to Mason as he jogged back. 'Keep running at them.'

After half-time, England quickly took charge, scoring two in five minutes. Declan, who had a yellow card against his name from the prior round, reminded

himself to tread carefully and not risk a suspension.
With the game wrapped up, Gareth took the safer
option and turned to his substitutes, giving Declan a
breather as he watched the latter stages from the bench.

Now expectations were sky-high, but Declan
tried not to think too far ahead, even if many
were predicting another comfortable England win
against Denmark. But there was a slightly nervous
atmosphere at Wembley as Declan walked out for the
anthems – and it only got tenser when Denmark took
the lead with a stunning free kick.

Suddenly, England looked flustered. It was the
first goal they had conceded at the tournament, but
Declan knew there was plenty of time to hit back.
He just settled himself down and focused on playing
the simple pass.

England got their equaliser before half-time, but
there was nothing to separate the teams in the second
half. The semi-final headed into extra time, and
Declan was soon watching with the rest of the players
and coaches from the bench as Gareth went with
fresh legs in midfield.

Then Raheem danced into the penalty area and fell as a Denmark defender closed in on him. 'Penalty!' Declan screamed along with tens of thousands of fans around him. The referee pointed to the spot and Harry sent England into the final, firing in the rebound after his penalty was saved.

Declan jogged onto the pitch to celebrate with his teammates. At the weekend, they would be playing in the Euro 2020 final!

After all the hugging, dancing and high-fiving, the England players turned their focus to the final against Italy. This would be their toughest game of the tournament, but they felt ready for it.

If Declan thought Wembley was rocking in the semi-final, it was even louder as the players walked out for the final. England were back in a major men's final for the first time in fifty-five years and a buzz of expectation filled the stadium.

Declan belted out the national anthem with his teammates and then tried to steady himself. It was normal to have nerves for this kind of game, and he just wanted to channel them into the type of all-action performance that England would need from him.

England got off to a dream start. From a quick attack down the right, a deep cross reached Luke Shaw at the back post, and he smashed a first-time shot off the post and into the net.

Declan was winning his battles, accepting the challenge of rattling an Italy midfield that had been dominant throughout the tournament. He pounced on every loose ball and cut off the passing angles between the lines.

But Italy clawed their way back into the game in the second half. Even as he scurried around to close down space, Declan could feel England dropping deeper and deeper. The Italians made it 1–1 and kept pushing for a second goal.

With fifteen minutes to go, Gareth turned to Jordan to try to restore control in midfield. Declan's heart sank when he saw his number on the assistant referee's electronic board, but he high-fived Jordan and Gareth as he left the pitch. He wished he could have stayed on and given even more for his teammates.

It came down to a penalty shootout and Declan's

stomach was doing somersaults. His legs felt shaky as he walked around the huddle of England players, guzzling water and preparing for penalties. He wasn't sure what to say and didn't want to affect their focus, so he just patted a few of the penalty takers on the back.

The shootout ended in tears. Jordan Pickford made two great saves, but England only scored two of their five penalties. As Italy celebrated wildly in one corner of the stadium, Declan and his teammates sank to the ground. Gareth and the coaches were quickly on the pitch to console the players – and, while still dealing with his own disappointment, Declan rushed over to support those who had missed their penalties and were feeling even greater heartbreak.

Back in the dressing room, Declan took off his boots and socks. There was silence all around. The trophy had been within touching distance and the emotions were still so raw. Eventually, Gareth walked to the front of the room and looked around at his players.

Declan could see that the shootout had been just as painful for his manager, who had his own history of missing a penalty at a major tournament.

'Lads, I know there are no words to take away the sting right now, but I'm incredibly proud of what you've achieved over the past month,' Gareth said. 'You went toe-to-toe with the best teams in the world and we're going to keep improving. Once the dust settles, the World Cup in Qatar is only eighteen months away. Trust me, the rest of the world knows that we mean business now.'

Declan knew Gareth was right. He wasn't ready to move past the pain of the final just yet, but there was a lot to look forward to and England had an exciting future.

CHAPTER 24

EUROPA LEAGUE EXCITEMENT

'Let's get off to a flier tonight,' Declan said, giving a fist bump to Michail and Jarrod as they all warmed up. The start of a new season always got the juices flowing, with the smell of the freshly cut pitches in the summer sun.

The thrill of playing in Europe was real, and tonight's battle against Dinamo Zagreb was one of the first stops on the Europa League journey.

Michail put West Ham ahead in the first half, but Declan could feel the tempo changing after half-time. It was time to take matters into his own hands.

Tracking back across midfield, Declan spotted his opportunity. The Dinamo right back pushed forward and clipped a pass back inside. But Declan read it, guessing correctly and darting in to intercept it. He raced forward down the left wing, leaving one defender stumbling.

Declan looked up and saw no support in the box. Michail was trying to catch up, but Declan knew there was no time to wait. He kept going, found himself in the box and then trusted his left foot to drill in a low shot from a tight angle. It was perfectly placed, zipping through the goalkeeper's legs and into the net. *2–0!*

Gooooooooooooooooooooaaaaaaaaaaaaaaaaalllllllllllllllll llllllllllllll!!!!!!!!!!!!!!!!!!!!!

He skipped over to the section of West Ham supporters and stopped in front of them, spreading his arms wide as the fans cheered and hugged.

The belief was flowing through the dressing room, and David continued to urge Declan to lead the way. With the way the team was playing, it was easy to forget how narrowly they had avoided relegation two years ago. Manchester City, Liverpool and Chelsea were all powering ahead at the top of the Premier

League table, but there was an opening for others to crash the party.

'It's still early days but I really think we could join you guys in the top four,' Declan said when he called Mason one evening. With Manchester United, Arsenal and Tottenham all struggling, West Ham surged onwards.

Declan was captaining the team even more these days, and his usual brand of relentless play was spreading throughout the team. Trailing in the FA Cup and staring at a major upset against Kidderminster, Declan refused to give up – and his teammates were right there with him.

In stoppage time, he laid the ball off and then backed himself to make one more run behind the Kidderminster defence. The pass from Pablo was right into his path and he kept his cool, cutting inside onto his right foot and blasting an unstoppable shot into the roof of the net. *1–1!*

Goooooooooooooooooooaaaaaaaaaaaaaaaaallllllllllllll llllllllllll!!!!!!!!!!!!!!!!!!!!!

He shimmied over the West Ham fans, with the

stadium scoreboard showing ninety-one minutes. When Jarrod won the tie with one of the last kicks of extra time, it was yet another example of the growing spirit in the dressing room.

That belief was on full display as Declan provided the spark for wins over Liverpool, Tottenham and Chelsea – though he did have to put up with Mason reminding him about the goal he scored against West Ham.

They were still battling in the Europa League too, surging into the semi-finals but falling just short. Competing in the Premier League and the Europa League seemed to catch up with the players in the final months of the season. Declan even felt it in his own performances, with his legs feeling heavier and more little knocks to battle through. It was tough to take, as managing just one win from their last seven Premier League games proved costly. West Ham would eventually finish seventh and qualify for the Europa Conference League action for next year.

After a gripping 2–2 draw against Manchester City, the eventual Premier League champions, in the final home game of the season, Declan was in the mood to unwind. It was almost six o'clock and the West Ham fans had long since left the stands. A few hours earlier, cheers and chants had been echoing around the London Stadium, especially when West Ham took a 2–0 lead.

But now, as Declan Rice trotted back down the tunnel, there was an eerie silence. 'Alright, let's do it!' he called over his shoulder, waving his hand hurriedly.

Following just behind him was what might have looked like the West Ham Under-6 squad. Four boys and two girls in a mix of West Ham kits and tracksuits raced across the greenest of green grass, smiling at each other in disbelief.

'Uncle Dec, this is… it's… wow!' shouted one of his nephews, struggling to find the right words. He just spun around in a slow circle, taking in the whole stadium.

Declan grinned. 'You're a Premier League footballer for the next fifteen minutes,' he said. He took the ball that had been tucked under his arm and dropped it at his feet. 'Well, if you can get the ball off me, that is!'

In a flash, little arms and legs sprang into action, rushing towards Declan as he dribbled away down the right wing.

'Get him!' screamed one of the girls, giggling.

Declan tapped the ball from his right foot to his left foot, dancing away from one of the tiny tacklers. He felt an ache in his leg – a reminder of the fierce ninety minutes he had just played against some of the top midfielders in the world. A quick change of direction left two of the boys on the ground amid more shrieks of laughter.

Finally, all six little ones caught up with him and, through a combination of clinging onto Declan's legs and diving on top of the ball, they did it!

A couple of the West Ham ground staff, who had been watching from the other half of the pitch, clapped loudly to everyone's surprise. Declan had got to know them well during his time at the club. 'Come on, surely you lads are on my side?!' he joked, spreading his arms out to make his point.

Declan then lay down on the pitch, pretending to be angry that the kids had won back the ball but

unable to hide the wide grin on his face. Then, as
the children celebrated their successful mission, he
quietly stood up, sneaked over and took the ball back
– and the game began all over again, just at a slightly
slower pace.

This was the life, Declan thought. All the excitement
and exhaustion of a Premier League weekend, followed
by this quality time with his nephews and their friends.
He knew that none of the children would stop talking
about this moment for the next few weeks.

With all the highs and lows of a typical season
swirling around him, it was sometimes easy to lose
sight of the simple things that brought him joy. That's
what had given Declan the idea of bringing the
youngsters onto the pitch that evening. He saw the
same glint of excitement in their eyes that he always
seemed to have in the old photos of him at that age
– and the same glint that he probably still had today
whenever he stepped onto the pitch in front of the
West Ham fans.

As he weaved between sliding tackles, Declan got
flashbacks to his own childhood – the football battles

in the street, the highs and lows of academy life
and his first steps as a professional. He was still just
twenty-three and, while he had packed a lot into those
years, Declan knew he was still just getting started.
He promised himself that he would be back with a
bang next season.

CHAPTER 25

A BRIGHT
FUTURE

The summer was finally here, and Declan knew that he needed to switch off from football now more than ever before. He had a feeling that he should treasure some calm before whatever came next.

Yes, he still had big decisions to make, with West Ham offering him a new contract and other clubs reportedly desperate to sign him. The attention was flattering, even if his family enjoyed teasing him about the £150 million price tag that had popped up in the headlines. It had not escaped his notice that one of the teams linked with him was Chelsea, and that brought back all kinds of thoughts and memories.

The appeal of the Champions League was very real,

but he was still in the early years of his career. He and his family had formed such a strong bond with West Ham, and he was already on the way to forming a lasting legacy at the club. Plus, to add to the big moments ahead, the 2022 World Cup in Qatar was on the horizon too.

He knew there was an extra level that he could unlock next season, with more shots, assists and goals. As he had discussed with David Moyes and the coaching staff last week, there were still little tweaks that he could make to his game that would help him take the big step from star to superstar.

But all of that could wait. Declan was overdue for a proper break and, for now, he just wanted some more time with Lauren, his family and his friends. As he packed a bag and prepared to leave Premier League life behind for a few weeks, he already felt more relaxed.

'Beach, here we come!' he shouted, adding swimming shorts to the pile. 'If I'm going to have the best season of my life next year, I need a nice tan!'

DECLAN RICE HONOURS

England
🏆 UEFA European Football Championship Finalist: 2020

Individual
🏆 Republic of Ireland U17 Player of the Year: 2016
🏆 West Ham United Young Player of the Year: 2016–17, 2017–18, 2018–19
🏆 FAI Young International Player of the Year: 2018
🏆 West Ham United Player of the Year: 2019–20, 2021–22
🏆 UEFA Europa League Squad of the Season: 2021–22

RICE

41 THE FACTS

NAME: Declan Rice

DATE OF BIRTH: 14 January 1999

PLACE OF BIRTH: Kingston upon Thames

NATIONALITY: English

BEST FRIEND: Mason Mount

CURRENT CLUB: West Ham

POSITION: CDM

THE STATS

Height (cm):	185
Club appearances:	198
Club goals:	10
Club assists:	10
Club trophies:	0
International appearances:	28
International goals:	2
International trophies:	0
Ballon d'Ors:	0

★ ★ ★ HERO RATING: 85 ★ ★ ★

GREATEST MOMENTS

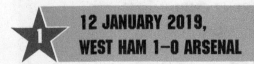

12 JANUARY 2019, WEST HAM 1–0 ARSENAL

Halfway through his second season in the West Ham starting line-up, Declan finally scored his first senior goal for the club, and what a goal it was. Early in the second half, he whipped a first-time shot into the top corner to win the London derby for West Ham and earn him the Player of the Match award too.

25 MARCH 2019, MONTENEGRO 1–5 ENGLAND

Just six weeks after Declan's switch from Ireland to England, Gareth Southgate picked him to start in this Euro 2020 qualifier. On his full debut, Declan put in an energetic display in defensive midfield, winning the ball back and launching attacks for his new national team. It was a sign of exciting things to come.

17 JULY 2020, WEST HAM 3–1 WATFORD

At the end of a difficult season, this was the day when West Ham showed they deserved to be in the Premier League. Michail Antonio got the first goal, Tomáš Souček scored the second, and Declan finished things off with a screamer from thirty yards. Phew – with the help of their inspiring young leader, the Hammers were staying up!

11 JULY 2021, ENGLAND 1–1 ITALY (LOST 3–2 ON PENALTIES)

Although this Euro 2020 final ended in a painful penalty defeat for England, it was still a huge and very proud moment for Declan. Together with his terrific teammates, he had made it all the way to a major international final, and got so close to glory. 'The last five weeks I've had the best time of my entire life,' Declan tweeted afterwards.

16 SEPTEMBER 2021, DINAMO ZAGREB 0–2 WEST HAM

After scoring the goal to send West Ham into the Europa League, Declan then scored this stunning solo goal on his debut in the competition. After winning the ball back, he dribbled all the way from his own half into the Dinamo Zagreb box, before sliding a shot through the keeper's legs. West Ham were off to a winning start and Declan was looking more dangerous than ever.

PLAY LIKE YOUR HEROES

WIN THE BALL BACK
LIKE DECLAN RICE

STEP 1: You're full of box-to-box energy, but don't forget to hold your position. Although it's tempting to rush forward and join every attack, your main job is to be your team's defensive midfielder. That means staying disciplined and staying back. Most of the time, anyway…

STEP 2: As the captain, it's also your job to communicate and lead by example. When your opponents have the ball, keep talking to your teammates, encouraging and organising them on the pitch.

STEP 3: Okay – time to win that ball back. Use your football brain to read the game and your energy to always be in the right place at the right time. Wherever the pass is going, you need to be there too, and before the player you're marking if possible!

STEP 4: If that doesn't work, use your strength, determination, patience and intelligence to track back and time your tackle to perfection.

STEP 5: Ball won back! Right – now it's time for you to decide what to do with it next. If you find yourself surrounded by opponents, it's best to play a simple pass to one of your (slightly) more skilful teammates.

STEP 6: But if you find yourself with lots of space in front of you, go for it! Dribble the ball forward as far as you can and then stay calm and find a way to finish things off, whether that's with a stylish pass or a powerful shot. GOAL!

TEST YOUR KNOWLEDGE

QUESTIONS

1. Which family member helped Declan to get a trial at the Chelsea academy?

2. Which future best friend and England teammate did Declan first meet at that trial?

3. How many goals did Declan score on his debut for the Grey Court School football team?

4. Which Chelsea legend gave Declan lots of advice and told him that he could call him 'JT'?

5. When Declan was released by Chelsea, which two other London clubs did he choose between?

6. Which West Ham manager handed Declan his first-team debut in May 2017?

7. Declan scored his first senior goal for West Ham against which club?

8. Which West Ham legend did Declan play alongside in midfield and later replace as captain?

9. True or false – Declan played for the England Under-21s?

10. At Euro 2020, Declan was a key part of the England midfield, alongside Mason Mount and which other player?

11. To what stage did Declan lead West Ham in the 2021–22 Europa League?

11. All the way to the semi-finals.
switching to play for the senior England team. 10. Kalvin Phillips.
9. False! He played for the Republic of Ireland at youth level, before
5. Fulham and West Ham. 6. Slaven Bilić. 7. Arsenal. 8. Mark Noble.
3. Three – he was a hat-trick hero! 4. John Terry.
1. His cousin, Taylor. 2. Mason Mount.